BACK IN THE BLUE HOUSE

BACK IN THE
BLUE HOUSE

JEFF GILES

TICKNOR & FIELDS
NEW YORK 1992

For information about permission to reproduce selections
from this book, write to Permissions, Ticknor & Fields,
215 Park Avenue South, New York, New York 10003.

Library of Congress Cataloging-in-Publication Data

Giles, Jeff.
Back in the blue house / Jeff Giles.
p.   cm.
ISBN 0-395-60843-0
I. Title.
PS3557.I3444B3   1992   91-28701
813'.54—dc20   CIP

Printed in the United States of America

AGM 10 9 8 7 6 5 4 3 2 1

With thanks for their support and encouragement: my sister,
Susan Heger, and my father, Glen Giles. Also, thanks to
Jennifer Bevill, Susan Schorr, Deborah Karl,
Andrew Wylie, John Herman, Caroline Sutton, Stacy Title,
Stephen Sherrill, James Wirth, Michael O'Donnell,
Melanie Thernstrom, and David Lipsky.

For my mother, Susan Ceci

In our house, there is only one bed,
too big for you, a little narrow for us both.

— Colette

I

JESUS, MARY, AND JOSEPH

"I ONLY MET Lincoln Hayes once, but as far as I could tell he was an absolute prick. When your father's grandfather died, Lincoln Hayes and his wife moved into his house. Your great-grandfather — he was such a sweetheart, Jeffrey, and he had more money than God. But no one would talk to him, you know? Your father wouldn't talk to him. Your grandfather wouldn't talk to him. I married your father and I thought, What the hell kind of family is *this* — no one talks to anybody else? Anyway, there was all this happy horseshit going on, so when your great-grandfather dies — why not, right? — he left everything to his maid. His maid's name was Abbey Hayes. She was married to Lincoln Hayes, and what a prick *he* was.

"One summer — you and Susan were six and eight — your father says, 'Let's go for a ride.' He was still a copilot for Mohawk, and he had just come home from a trip. So your father says, 'Let's go for a ride. Let's go look at my grandfather's house.' I mean, your father refused to drive me to that man's funeral. I'm in mourning on a fuckin' *bus*, and ten years later your father's feeling — what — sentimental?

"Well, we go for a ride. One of your father's famous memory-lane rides. When we get to your great-grandfather's house — Lincoln Hayes had been living there for years — there's an auction going on. There's twenty or

3

thirty people sitting on the lawn in folding chairs. Come to find out, Abbey Hayes had died and left everything to her husband. Then Lincoln Hayes had died and — needless to say — he had no one to leave anything to. So they were gonna auction off his estate, all of which had belonged to your great-grandfather, because the Hayeses had been piss-poor to begin with. They were gonna auction off the estate and send the money to Lincoln Hayes's *third* cousins. You know? Who were living in *Canada,* or something. I mean, Jesus, Mary, and Joseph, Jeffrey. They were gonna donate the land to the friggin' Boy Scouts.

"Anyway, I get out of the car. Your father says, 'Susan, what are you doing?' I say, 'I'm putting a stop to this happy horseshit.' He says, 'Get back in the car, woman.' I say, 'Glen, these things have been in your family — These things have been in the Giles family a hundred, a hundred fifty years. This stuff came over on *boats,* for Christ's sake.' Well, your father will not get out of the car. He has too much — I don't know — dignity. I'm thinking, Well, fuck you and the horse you rode in on, Glen. I mean, my family had nothing, Jeffrey. My mother, my father — they had *nothing*.

"So I get out of the car. The auctioneer's selling a piece of Dresden — a man and a woman playing chess. It's absolutely gorgeous and, so help me God, I *recognize* the thing. I say, 'Glen, you remember that?' He says, 'No. Get in the car.' I say, 'The hell you don't.' I walk across the lawn. I walk right up to the auctioneer and I say, 'Hand it over.' Needless to say, he looks at me like I'm a crazy lady. He says, 'Who are you?' I say, 'I'm Susan Giles. Don't you sell another fuckin' thing.'

"Five minutes later, the auctioneer and I are still going

at it. People are folding up their blankets, you know? People are *running* for their cars. Finally, a lawyer comes out of the house. He says, 'Who are you?' I say, 'I'm Susan Giles. These things belong to my husband's family.' 'Not anymore they don't.' Blah, blah, blah. This, that, and the other thing. I finally get ahold of the Dresden, and I say, 'These things belong to my husband. If he has to buy everything back a spoon at a time, he will.'

"Finally, the lawyer looks at me and says, 'Mrs. Giles, where *is* your husband?' I stop for a second. I say, 'He's in the car.' I mean, looking back, the whole friggin' thing was ridiculous. But what was I gonna do? 'He's in the car with the kids.' Everybody turns around. Your father is standing by the side of the car. He's got his airline uniform on and he is *pissed*. He's playing with his hat, you know? He's tapping his hat on the roof of the Ford. He looks at me and he says, 'Susan, get in the car.' There's this silence. Then the lawyer and the auctioneer — I couldn't believe the balls of these guys — they say, 'Get in the car, Susan.' So I think for a couple of seconds — your father is tapping his hat, you kids are in the back seat staring at me like I'm out of my mind — and I finally say, '*Fuck* it,' and I put down your great-grandfather's Dresden and I go."

In 1936, my mother was born into a world already piled high with more things than it had names for. A Webster's dictionary published when she was four includes the following entries under the heading "New Words": amphetamine, Bauhaus, bra, carcinogen, Dust Bowl, estrogen, FM, jive, leftist, microfilm, Nazism, parapsychology, pastrami, racism, station wagon, and video. When I imagine my mother at her beginnings, she appears in dim outline.

I see a young woman in the late 1950s. She has pale hands, thin lips, and — after the fashion of the day — a hairdo that springs up like a four-story building. The man she marries, my father, has joined the navy and is learning how to fly. He is handsome. He squints when he smiles. He is a man who wears a uniform at a time when uniforms are still pure and strange. It's hard to picture my father in this past incarnation. Like my mother, he appears as a thumbnail sketch, an unknown quantity waiting to be defined.

My mother's name — after a handful of divorces and separations — is again what it once was: Susan Ceci. Her parents, Ercole and Almerinda Ceci, were Italian immigrants. When I was young, I used to imagine my mother's birthplace, Warwick, Rhode Island, as a dark Old World city that smelled of salt water and machinery. I imagined it as a place where everybody bantered in the mother tongue, where the women rolled their eyes and wrung their hands, where the men had tufts of wiry chest hair that poked out from between their shirt buttons, where people sat out at night on an endless row of porches. Perhaps Warwick *had* been like that once. But years later, when I finally visited the city, I was terribly disappointed. Warwick had wide, blank highways, strip malls, and those tiny, boxy Fotomats that are plunked down in parking lots everywhere. Warwick was a generic no-place, a stopping point between other cities.

I have never been clear on how my grandparents wound up in Warwick. A few years ago, I met a woman whose family also had its beginnings in Italy and, finding a soul mate, she pulled at my hand excitedly and insisted on knowing what region my grandparents had emigrated from. I thought for a moment but found, to her amazement, that I didn't know. It was an embarrassing episode and it stayed with me for a while. Rather than ask my mother where her family was from — my mother does not traffic in such things as simple answers — I arbitrarily decided that my ancestors had come from the North.

What had Ercole and Almerinda's life been like in the North? I have no idea. I do know that their life in Warwick was much the same as my parents' life would be in New Hartford, New York. Like my mother, my grandmother spent much of her life attached to men whose love came like a collision — disorienting and brief. Eventually, my mother learned to avoid such meetings, to sidestep men she'd been unable to sidestep before. But Ercole was my grandmother's first collision. She hadn't yet learned to get out of the way.

My grandfather Ercole was a man possessed of what I believe are called ruined good looks, with a long, knobby body and a face creased and sunken like a relief map. He made shoes during the day and drank beer at night. When Ercole wandered in at two in the morning, he'd fall through the kitchen, stripping off his clothes and draping them over whatever he found in his path — an African violet, a gooseneck lamp. Eventually, he'd make it to the bedroom where Almerinda was sleeping. It was a simple room, with a nightstand and a burgundy throw rug. Over the bed, there was a crucifix covered with a transparent plastic bag. On the nightstand, there was a wooden Virgin Mary, a dish of pennies, buttons, and safety pins, and a set of rosary beads arranged in a dusty spiral. Ercole would arrive at the doorway — naked but for a pair of golden-toed black socks — and glower over the arc of his sleeping wife. Some nights, he would wake Almerinda and beat her. Other times, he would sink into a steady animal sleep.

In the morning, my mother would walk by the bedroom and the door would be ajar. Ercole would be unconscious — his hair in a black wash against the sheet, his right arm dangling down toward the floor. My mother would retrieve her father's clothes, which hung as if they had been blown into the branches of a tree. When she heard him turning over in bed, she would fill a glass with cold water, and carry it in to him. Ercole would sit up in bed and gulp the water down. His Adam's apple would bob; his eyes would shoot back in his head. After a few moments, he'd look at my mother and his face would dissolve in sweetness. He'd set the glass on the nightstand, hoist my mother onto the bed, and say, "Knock knock."

When my mother was in the tenth grade, her brothers Henry and Ricco were drafted into the Korean War. Her oldest brother, Peter, had a punctured eardrum and, after being passed over by the army, he took a job at a rubber company. Peter's and Ercole's salaries weren't enough to support the family so my mother and my Auntie Anna left school. Anna took on secretarial work, and my mother nine-to-fived in a shop that sold awnings. When Henry and Ricco returned from Korea, the army put them through college, and Peter eventually managed to pay his own way. My mother and Auntie Anna never went back to school. For many years, whenever she successfully pressed a pair of trousers, wrote a check, or hammered a nail, my mother would look at my sister and me with a tilted head and say, "Not bad for a tenth-grade education, right?"

Publicly, she seemed less comfortable with the fact that she had never graduated from high school. In her first years as an interior decorator, before she returned to school for a degree, my mother told her clients that she had attended the Rhode Island School of Design. She had, after all, grown up near the campus, and had a functional knowledge of the school's curriculum and geography.

"Jesus Christ, Jeffrey," she'd exclaim, when I pressed her on this point. "I dated enough *men* from RISD!"

My mother was the last child to leave her parents' house. During her final years there, Ercole and Almerinda spoke to each other only in phrases. They were like two passengers sharing a train compartment, each noticing only the other's bad taste in novels and his habit of sleeping with his mouth open. My mother watched her parents, always, from another room. She painted a little and wrote ceaselessly to Anna and Peter. She slept, worked, and picked Ercole's clothes up off the floor. All the while, she dreamt of the only thing there was to dream of: marriage. It was a peculiar fate, and my mother's generation, I think, was the last to be tied to it. They fled from one man's house to another's.

My father won my mother twice. Perhaps it is better put this way: my father won my mother from two different men.

In 1961, my father, Glen John Giles, was a navy lieutenant stationed at Quonset Point, Rhode Island. By the time my mother met him, she was already engaged to a cadet named James McAuliffe. I learned only recently of my mother's first fiancé. She mentioned him offhandedly one day, and when I expressed surprise she looked up from a cutting board, on which she had been chopping green peppers, and said, "I was *how old,* remember. I wanted to get out of the house. He was learning how to fly. What do you want to know?"

Confronted with this new information, I imagine my mother stretched out on a great, sprinkler-dampened lawn, watching cadets in whites and rifles go clicking by. I imagine her in a general store on a navy base, saluting comically to everyone she passes. On weekends, my mother told me, she and her friends went to the base to dance. The instant they got through the door, the cadets flew at them with petitions. They danced to "Havin' a Heat Wave," which dovetailed into "Too Darn Hot," and "Blue Moon," which dovetailed into "My Blue Heaven." The rooms were overheated and badly decorated, and everyone in the navy seemed to talk about the same things: the sublime clarinet solo, the grace of airplanes. All in all, it was a strange tour of duty. But this was how my mother — a descendant of Old World men, loud conversations, and stained tablecloths — met and fell in love with James McAuliffe. They dated a short time, and the night before he went to sea he asked her to marry him. My mother, sitting on her hands on the hood of his Plymouth, considered the offer a moment, then said, "Don't mind if I do."

Two weeks later, my mother met my father at a cocktail party. He was drinking with a friend of hers named Irene. He was drunk and had his feet up on a chair. My mother approached them, flattening her skirt with her hands.

"You could move your feet and I could sit down," my mother said.

My father looked at her. "Or you could go away," he said.

"Glen!" Irene said, lurching at him and pushing at his feet to no avail. "Susan, he's drunk."

"Yes, Susan, I'm drunk."

"I can see that. You're not exactly keeping it a secret."

Irene pulled at my father's legs again, this time knocking a glass off the arm of his chair. My father bent down to pick it up. After righting himself, he looked at my mother and said, "You again?"

My mother turned on her heel and stormed away. My father stood up, collected himself, and followed her. The party was crowded and as my mother zigzagged toward the ladies' room, my father barreled forward, shouting, "Excuse me, this girl's just stolen my wallet." My mother slipped into the rest room; my father leaned on the door. When my mother came out, he asked her for a date. When she told him she was engaged, he congratulated her, and asked her out again. Before long, he was courting her with the fervor of a man who must convince a woman to change her life. He made my mother feel uncertain and beautiful, and after a short time she was engaged to two men.

Later, long after they were married, my father told my mother that he regretted the frenzied pitch of their courtship. He told her that he should have fallen in and out of love with a dozen women before meeting her. He meant this as an apology, I suppose, for a marriage continually disrupted by anger and absence. Had circumstances been different in Quonset Point, he said, he would have set her up on a shelf. He would have told her he loved her and asked her to wait.

But my parents could not wait. One day, James Mc-Auliffe walked off a ship and searched the crowd for my mother, but couldn't find her.

When my father went to meet Ercole for the first time, Ercole was unconscious in bed. My father stood talking to my mother through a screen door. It was a Sunday morning and he held his hat in his hand like a tambourine.

"Listen," my mother said, fiddling with the doorknob, "you could meet Mama. Would you come say hi to Mama?"

"Anything for you, girlfriend," my father said.

My mother smiled and conveyed him to the parlor, holding a forefinger to her lips as they passed Ercole's bedroom.

Almerinda was sitting on a couch, crocheting. She was a big woman and the slack skin that hung down from her arms swayed as she worked. She must have spent a good deal of time crocheting. For years she presented us with afghans. Even after we had run out of beds and chairbacks to cover, the afghans kept arriving. They popped open like parachutes and descended onto refrigerators and television sets.

My mother made a few brisk introductions, then opened a window to dissipate the cloying smell of perfume and talcum. Almerinda, whose eyebrows were wide semicircles drawn with an umber marker, paused in her work and looked my father over. She surveyed his navy uniform, his clean, straight topcoat, his crew cut.

"Jesus God, what a funny head!" she said.

"Mama!"

"Sorry," Almerinda said, wincing.

"They keep our hair a bit short, Mrs. Ceci. Cuts down on the wind resistance."

"Sorry?"

"A little joke, ma'am."

"I see. A pilot joke."

"That's right."

There was a pause. "Come here. Let me touch it."

"I'm sorry?"

"Your hair."

"Mama, you are *amazing* me!"

"It's like dead grass or something."

"Go right ahead, Mrs. Ceci."

"Glen!"

My father stepped up and bowed; Almerinda touched his hair with the tips of her fingers.

How much did my mother know about my father? She knew he was of Irish and English descent. She knew that he was an only child, that he had been born in Providence, and brought up in Hanover, New Hampshire. She knew that he had studied architecture at Cornell under full scholarship, but that after a string of bad semesters he was invited to leave and left. She knew he wore his Cornell sweatshirt inside out — a symbol, he claimed, of that fall from grace.

My mother had met my grandmother Louise and thought her eccentric. "One minute you're talking to her," she told her friends, "and the next minute it's like she's getting messages from outer space." Of his father, Sidney, my father never uttered a word, so my mother had only her hunches: that Sidney had died, possibly in a car, possibly in a bed, and that his death had come as a shock.

13

Three weeks before my parents were to be married, my father disclosed that his father was alive. He put my mother in a car and drove her to New Hampshire. When I was in college, I drove from Rhode Island to New Hampshire many times. It is a five-hour trip, made predominantly on winding, one-lane roads. For some reason, I associate it with winter, when the trees are frozen and you can feel your muscles knot up beneath your clothes. On this particular trek, my father clutched the steering wheel to his chest and drove agonizingly slowly. My mother did not say a word. She scratched her head, and absentmindedly opened and closed the glove compartment. She stared at the road and waited for my father to speak.

"Look, Susan," he said a few hours into New Hampshire, "I'd rather you didn't — If my father offers you a glass of water or something, I'd rather you didn't take it."

"A glass of water?"

"Or whatever. You know, 'Do you want to use the telephone?' I'm just trying to make a point."

"About what?"

"About — Look, why don't we just stop right now and get you a drink?"

"This is ridiculous, Glen. I'm not even thirsty."

"Good. Then there won't be a problem."

My grandfather Sidney is a mild, steady man. When my father was a child, he was in the restaurant supply business. When I was a child, he was selling *World Book* encyclopedias. He never found a career that suited him, and the family never had any money to speak of. He mowed his lawn twice a week in summer and kept an immaculate garden; he rolled his pant legs up his calves, buckled his belt on the side, played gin rummy, and drank Dr. Pepper. He never plotted to make a million dollars, and he never did.

My grandmother Louise was an alcoholic. Occasionally, she was violent — she would pull down a bookcase or smash the living room table with my father's parade rifle. Other times, she would simply sit in the kitchen after dinner, drinking, and holding forth with a barrage of exquisite and pointless lies. Her husband would be out in the backyard, and she'd shout, "Sidney! Someone's stolen the car!" Sidney would rush in and find it exactly where he had left it in the driveway. He'd give Louise a furious look, but she'd merely shake her head and say, "Kids out for a quick joyride."

For a long time, it surprised me that my father had been closer to Louise than to Sidney. He'd inherited Sidney's features, his squint, his disinclination to talk about himself, his habit of staring at his fingernails while he spoke. I couldn't imagine what he shared with Louise. Eventually, I came to understand something that my father had understood for some time: that Louise's intrigues were a kind of a domestic terrorism, a rebuttal to the life she shared with Sidney. After all, my grandparents' marriage was surely not as simple as I have described it. A man who gardens, a woman who pulls down bookcases: this is what a child sees, a child who knows nothing of cause and effect, and has no idea what drives a man one way and a woman the other.

Once, when I was very young, my mother threw my father out of the house. It was late at night and he had just arrived home. He had a cast on his right arm and was sitting, crying, in the dim yellow light at the top of the stairs. My mother was tearing through the house in a rage. From my room, I could hear her calling the police and, a little bit later, I heard my father retreat down the stairs and out of the house. I was five years old and I had no idea what my parents were fighting about. Still, for years I carried around this strange image of my mother: here was a woman who sent her husband away in the middle of the night, in the middle of winter. When he had broken his arm. When he was crying.

Shortly after my father's nineteenth birthday, Sidney left Louise to marry a woman named Liz. She was six years younger than my grandmother and worked with Sidney at the restaurant supply company. According to my mother, the consequences of Sidney and Liz's marriage came quickly. My father stopped speaking to Sidney. Sidney's father stopped speaking to Sidney. Sidney and Liz got fired.

Later — long after these feuds had disintegrated and new ones had sprung up to take their place — I would visit my grandfather and Granny Liz at their new home on McCommas Boulevard in Dallas. Liz was the first person I ever knew who collected books, and I remember being astonished by the sheer mass of them. Wall after wall in their home was filled ceiling to floor with thick, dark bindings. The titles — *Middlemarch*, *The Human Comedy*, *Can You Forgive Her?* — meant nothing to me. After all, I had grown up poring over Cinderella-style sports stories like *The Catcher with the Glass Arm* and, a little later, books about teenagers with psychic powers. Of the afternoons we spent in Dallas, I remember the smell of Dove soap and the sight of Sidney — still handsome with his spindly legs and his startlingly white knee-socks — darting around the tennis court. Of the evenings, just the dull glow of a black and white television and everywhere the smell of books.

My parents arrived in Hanover, New Hampshire, at six in the evening, and the first thing Liz did was offer my mother a glass of water. Without waiting for an answer, she hurried off to the kitchen. When she returned a minute later, no one had spoken.

"Here you go, Susan," Liz said, handing her the glass. "It's just from the tap."

"That's fine," my mother said. My father glared at her.

The group then retired to the living room where, for half an hour or so, nothing much was said. They discussed plans for my parents' wedding; they discussed the ice on the roads. Most of the time, though, Sidney sat in his chair, sucked his pipe, and sent streams of sweet-smelling smoke across the room to Liz. Liz reclined on the couch, lit cigarettes end to end and sent a wall of smoke back at Sidney. After an hour, my father stood and stretched. My mother followed him out of the house, leaving her glass to soak a white ring into the table. Later, Liz would come across the glass and see that it had not been touched.

My parents were married for more or less the same period that the Beatles were together. Their wedding took place in June of 1962, and my sister, Susan Karen Giles, was born about the time *Please Please Me* was released. My own birth, in 1965, was sandwiched between *Help!* and *Rubber Soul*. This discography of my parents' relationship does not yield much, unfortunately. What I know about my mother and my father rarely intersects with what I know about the times they have lived in. A couple of years ago, by way of experiment, I played them both "I Want to Hold Your Hand," and each insisted that they had never heard it before.

The home movies taken at my parents' wedding are quite jumpy, and no one manages to stay in view very long. My father and mother appear at the exit of a tall Providence church, shake the hand of their priest, Father Donovan, and then walk out among a crowd of naval officers and Italians. The newlyweds seem embarrassed. They nod too much; they look discreetly for their car. Some time passes, the camera flits around. When it settles on my parents again, they are still looking for their car. It is as if someone has, for a joke, parked it half a mile away. In any case, my parents walk and walk.

The only record I have seen of my parents' reception is a small black-and-white snapshot. In it, my parents are standing in front of a cake, which is set atop a collapsible TV tray. The cake is two-tiered and topped with a lacy, heart-shaped arch. To my parents' left stand Ercole and Almerinda. To their right, Sidney and his ex-wife, Louise. Louise, who looks like Eudora Welty here, wears pearly cat's-eye glasses and has a silk jacket draped over her shoulders. Sidney's bow tie is crooked — it tilts down toward the floor like an airplane propeller just starting to turn. My father is looking at the camera; my mother is looking at her shoes.

It is hard to say from the photograph where the reception took place. On the ceiling above the wedding party hangs a fishing net, filled with sand dollars, starfish, and coral. On the wall behind them, a mounted wide-mouth bass is partially visible. All I really know about this reception is that because of Ercole and Louise's twin predilection for alcohol, my parents did not serve liquor. As it happened, Louise arrived drunk and, after an hour, was given a naval escort home.

For the first five or six years of their marriage, my father was a junior copilot with Mohawk Airlines, and we lived in a series of rented homes in upstate New York. The houses were bleak and barely furnished. By necessity, they were near airports. Often, they were near little else. My only memory of these times is that, in winter, the snow seemed to pile up higher than the house.

In 1968, my parents bought a home at 10 Gilbert Road in New Hartford. The house sat on a one-and-a-half-acre plot, which was dotted with rare varieties of trees and bordered on two sides by woods. Years later, when my father decided I was strong enough to push a mower, he took me into the backyard and pulled the cord on our John Deere. He then gestured toward the lawn, which at my age looked inconceivably large — like a vast tract of Canadian wilderness — and returned through the French doors to his airline schedules and his trip-bidding forms. I struggled with the mower, the handle of which came nearly to my throat. I had no idea how one mowed a lawn. It didn't occur to me, for instance, to mow in straight, parallel lines. Instead, I would mow in circles and high tufts of grass would dart up behind me as I passed. When I became bored with one particular patch of the lawn — mowing around the swingset was especially tedious — I would simply drag the mower fifty feet and start up again. To anyone watching, it would have appeared not so much that I was mowing the lawn as giving it a bad haircut. I would occasionally look in at my father, but his back would be turned. My father had a sink-or-swim approach to life.

My father has always been a swimmer. He loves to hear the perfect hum of a fan belt he has just replaced, or to consider the sharp greens and blues of a television that has only recently lain in pieces on the living room floor. However, there are those of us who, upon finding ourselves unprepared and in unknown waters, would simply rather sink. I have always found there to be something relaxing about sheer failure. About throwing one's hands up, about abandoning projects in a huff. About misplacing that one bolt without which a blender, say, positively cannot function.

In 1973, although I was strong enough to push a mower, I had difficulty starting one. My mother lived in constant fear that I would have an accident while mowing — losing not a finger or a toe, but a leg — and she monitored me from a second-story window. When the mower stalled, I would yank at the cord for a minute or so. Then, convinced I was about to dislocate my shoulder, I would slump down onto the grass. Eventually, my mother would come padding out of the house in her pink corduroy robe, and while my father's back was turned, the two of us would alternate in our attempts to revive the machine. Often this went on into dusk.

The house at 10 Gilbert Road was originally built by the owner of the area's largest supermarket chain for his newlywed daughter and her husband. Progress on it must have been slow, however, because the daughter had divorced and fled the state before it was completed. The project, once a labor of love, became a white elephant. The supermarket owner had construction finished in a hurry, with whatever materials were on hand. The result was a house that was by turns elegant and plain — a house with a few bright, open rooms and a few cloistered, dank ones; a house with fine oak floors and crumbling cork ceilings. My father began renovating the place as soon as we moved in. He repaneled bedrooms; he plastered ceilings. His chief glory, though, was the grooved maple mantel above the fireplace in the living room. In my wallet, I carry a photograph of my father in his Mohawk uniform. He is resting his arm on the mantel and smiling. Fifteen years later, it appears to be a photograph of my father but, at the time it was taken, it was a photograph of the mantel.

In the early seventies, my father had little seniority with Mohawk Airlines and was obliged to accept whatever trips were offered him. He'd be home with us in New Hartford for a week, then away for two weeks, and so on. At the time, my father was driving a forest green Ford station wagon, and I remember being surprised and thrilled whenever I found it parked in the driveway. Our family could only afford one car and my father liked to buy giant ones. After the Ford came a dull gold '72 Cadillac — a car so big that its body heaved up and down on its chassis, and it required four or five points to make a three-point turn. While my father's car was parked in the employee lot at the Syracuse airport, my mother was left behind at 10 Gilbert Road without any means of transportation. My father told her, "You could drop me off," but he knew she couldn't. For as long as my father had been buying big cars, my mother had been terrified of driving them.

Separated from her own family, my mother soon undertook to reconstruct my father's. At this point, relations were still strained between my father and his father, Sidney — not surprising, given that Louise was an avid practitioner of the guilt trip and sulked with abandon whenever she suspected my father had seen his stepmother, Liz. Relations between Sidney and my great-grandfather were nonexistent. Gramps, as he was known to the family, had never forgiven Sidney for divorcing Louise and marrying a younger woman, although he had done it himself. He felt humiliated by the failure of his son's marriage. In fact, when he heard Louise was planning to return to upstate New York to live — to flaunt the fact of her divorce in front of his oldest friends — he offered her $1,000 to stay away. She did not.

I don't know much about Gramps, aside from the fact that he cut Sidney out of his will and had "more money than God." My mother visited him on occasion and he cherished her visits. He told her she was an angel and loaded her up with gifts. My father returned the presents — out of loyalty to his father, amazingly. Here, then, is how matters stood: My father was not talking to Sidney. Gramps was not talking to Sidney. My father was not talking to Gramps because Gramps was not talking to Sidney.

The day before Gramps died, my mother was with him in the hospital. "He was the sweetest man in the world, Jeffrey," she has told me. "He was holding my hand, and he was going on and on about something — I don't know what — and I interrupted him. I said, 'Listen, Gramps, I don't want to upset you, but I brought Sidney with me.' Well, Gramps ignores me and just goes on talking. So I stop him again. I say, 'Gramps, I want you to see your son.' Well, he gets all quiet for a minute, then he says, 'Susan, you're such an angel. For you, I'll see him.' So Sidney comes in and he's looking at the floor, you know, and

Gramps is looking at the ceiling. Well, finally they look at each other. Jeffrey, I wish you could have been there — it was like a movie or something. Gramps just gasps and says, 'Sidney,' and Sidney gasps and says *'Dad.'*"

Gramps died within days, and everything he owned went to his maid, Abbey Hayes. Against my father's wishes, my mother went to speak with her. The two of them sat Indian-style on a porch and my mother explained that Gramps and Sidney had reconciled a day earlier and that Gramps had intended to change his will. Mrs. Hayes — an elderly woman who had long praised Gramps's generosity — said, "Yes, of course." Two weeks later, however, she died of heart failure and the money went to her disagreeable husband, Lincoln. Against my father's wishes, my mother went to speak with him. My mother sat Indian-style on the porch and Mr. Hayes paced around her. My mother explained the situation to him, but he would not be moved. In desperation, she offered to buy back the family's silver, all of which was engraved with curling, Old English Gs, but Lincoln Hayes sent her packing.

Years later, as we drove away from the auction at my great-grandfather's house, my parents fought and my sister, Susan, hummed at the top of her lungs. Drifting in and out of sleep, I heard only isolated snatches of the argument. My father wanted my mother to stop meddling in his family's affairs. Didn't she have a mother? Didn't she have a father? Half an hour from New Hartford, it began pouring down rain and the station wagon hydroplaned and went off the road. When my father saw that no one was hurt, he turned off the engine, opened his door, and disappeared into the rain. Furious, my mother got behind the wheel. She started the engine, then — remembering her fear of the giant car — turned it off again and slumped down in the seat. Twenty minutes later, a state policeman arrived and, assuming we had broken down, radioed for a truck to tow us home.

A week after this incident, my mother's father died and my mother bought a car. Ercole had been hospitalized for what the doctors believed was a liver condition brought on by his drinking. Surgery was performed in an operating room kept cold to minimize the risk of infection. It turned out that nothing was wrong with Ercole's liver, but six days later he died of pneumonia.

As for the car, it was a dull-red Volkswagen Bug — a damaged tomato of a thing with a trunk where the engine should have been. My mother would stuff the trunk to its breaking point and, inevitably, it would burst open on some stretch of highway. The hood would slap up against the windshield, and we'd turn to watch our clothes — first forming a tall, bright column in the air, then raining down behind us in the road. My father — his patriotic soul bristling at the prospect of a foreign automobile — said he couldn't stand the sight of the Volkswagen, and my mother told him, "So don't look at it."

Earlier, I mentioned a night when my mother turned my father out of the house, and I said that, at the time, I was too young to understand the nature of their argument. I should also add that, as a child, I habitually fled from the scenes of my parents' disputes. They took place in the kitchen more often than not, and from my room upstairs I heard only the knocking over of chairs and the harsh, indecipherable rhythm of my parents' voices. My slightly older sister — a rather excitable, unpredictable girl frequently seen storming through rooms, waving her hands in the air, and shouting, "*Oh* my God! *Oh* my God!" — would race headlong down the stairs and throw herself into the fight. I don't know if she understood what the arguments were about, and we've never talked about the scenes she witnessed in the kitchen at 10 Gilbert Road and, later, in the kitchen of our house in Cohasset, Massachusetts. Knowing my sister, though, I imagine she flung herself at my father and shouted, "Stop fighting. Stop fuckin' fighting!"

"Susan Karen, watch your language!"

"Glen, you've got some fucking nerve!"

"Stop fuckin' fighting!"

"Language, goddammit! *Language!*"

Once, when my sister was away, my parents had a particularly bad go-around. Upstairs, my heart racing, I lay on my bed and cried. I listened to the thumping of furniture for an hour and a half — fearing all the while that without my sister to break up the argument it would roar on indefinitely — and then I tiptoed down the stairs and out the front door. Outside, I could hear my parents' voices still, and knew that everyone on the block could too. My parents' fights were unabashedly public; waiting them out, I always careened between fear and humiliation.

I circled around to the back of the house, and looked in through the kitchen window. I suppose I wanted to make sure that my father wasn't hurting my mother, although I don't know what, as an eight-year-old, I could have done about it if he was. Looking inside, I saw that a bag of flour had fallen off the counter and that my parents were kicking it around the room. The bag had torn open and their clothes and their hands and their hair were covered with a bright white dust.

Two months later, while coming in from school, I stumbled through a plate glass door. My mother rushed me to the emergency room where I was given twelve stitches in my right elbow. When I had finally fallen asleep that night, my mother called Mohawk Crew Scheduling and asked them where my father was. Crew Scheduling told her they had no idea. They told her that he wasn't working and that, as far as the airline knew, he was at home in New Hartford. When my father came home a few days later, my mother confronted him and there was a row. My mother rarely called Crew Scheduling after that. When she did, they would confirm that her husband was on a trip but regret that they didn't know where.

Soon, my father became a captain. He complimented other captains on their landings, and laughed about being paid to fly people around. My father had a new vocabulary: Leaving was "departure." Returning was "deadheading." A night away from home was an "R.O.N." And dinner time was "1800." He had abandoned "Yes" and all its subtle variants — "Afraid so," "Of course," "Why not?" — in favor of "That's affirmative." And, before answering a question, my father had begun pausing for ten or fifteen seconds. It was clear that he had heard the question, and eventually he would answer it. Still, for years, my father always seemed to be thinking about something else.

"You know, Jeffrey, I can't remember a lot of the guys I dated before your father, but I remember every friggin' stewardess he ever fucked around with. Excuse me —

every *flight attendant.* Sherrie Wegman was the first. We're married five years and all of a sudden your father's coming home with recipes. You know? And *advice.* 'Oh, Susan, here's how you get those rust stains off the sink.' You've got to be pretty screwed up, right? You got to *want* somebody to know, if you're bragging about it like that. Jesus, Mary, and Joseph. Well, I did not know. I thought — with God as my witness — I thought that he wouldn't commit adultery because he was Catholic. With God as my witness. My family fought and this and that, but we were *very* Catholic. It was only when I met your father and the Gileses that I realized the word was meaningless. Anyway, I thought he wouldn't commit adultery because he was Catholic. Well, I was nuts. I mean, that shows you, that really *shows* you how screwed up I was at the time. Because I was screwed up for a lot of years. You were too young to remember — you ask your sister. You'd say, 'When's Daddy coming home?' And I'd be thinking, 'Fucked if I know, kid.'

"When I figured out about Sherrie — so help me God — I called her mother. I mean, I'm *married* to this man. I've got two of this man's children. I was not going to let this go on. So I call Sherrie's mother. Because I confront your father and he says, 'Susan, Susan, what are you *talking* about? You're acting *paranoid.*' I figure what have I got to lose, right? So I call Sherrie's mother. I say, very nicely, because I was a sweet girl then . . . You laugh, Jeffrey, but it's true. I say, 'Mrs. Wegman, your daughter is going at it with my husband.' Of course, she thinks I'm out of my mind. She hangs up. I call her back. I say, 'Look, Mrs. Wegman, this is nothing against your daughter, who I'm sure is very nice, but she's fucking my husband.' She hangs up. I call back. I say, 'Mrs. Wegman, is your daughter dating a pilot named Glen Giles? And does he drive a forest green Ford station wagon, license plate MOHAWK 2? Yes or no?' What's she going to say? She's *seen* the car. Well, she gives me some b.s. — this, that, and the other thing —and she hangs up. But two weeks later, your father has stopped seeing Sherrie Wegman.

"Six months go by, and I meet this guy, Anthony, at the horse track. At Suffolk Downs. My friend Leslie and I used to watch the races. Oh, Jeffrey, why the hell not? Don't be such a prude your whole life. Anyway, come to find out, Anthony knows everybody at the track. He knows the owners. He sits with them at the top of the bleachers. Every so often he comes down and flirts with us and says, 'Listen, girls, put ten dollars on Tough Customer in the second,' and we would. And Tough Customer would win. By five, ten yards. The other horses are *falling down*. Come to find out, the track is totally rigged. I was shocked. But Leslie and I must have made two, three hundred dollars this way. Pretty soon, it's obvious that this guy is coming on to me. I say, 'Anthony' — he was Italian and he was actually a sweet, sweet guy — I say, 'Anthony, see this ring on my finger? If you think I'm getting involved with you, you got another think coming.' So Anthony says — I'll never forget this — 'But, Susan, your husband is seeing that stewardess lady. I see them together all the time.' I say, 'Anthony, you son of a bitch, that's a lot of happy horseshit.'

"Two weeks later, Leslie and I are at the track and Anthony comes prancing down the bleachers. He says, 'Hello, girls.' We say, 'Hello, Anthony.' He says, 'Susan, come with me. I want to show you something.' We go for a

ride. Come to find out, Anthony has been following your
father around for days. He says, 'Susan, Sherrie Wegman's
mother lives two miles from here and your husband's station wagon is sitting in her driveway.' I say, 'Anthony, if
you're bullshitting me . . .' Anyway, we pull up. Your father's car is not there. Anthony swears up and down that it
was there. Tells me the license plate. Tells me there were a
couple of two-by-fours sticking out the back. Tells me your
father was wearing a red sweatshirt but he couldn't read it
because it was inside out. I'm thinking, This guy's got no
reason to lie. I mean, granted, he's trying to get me into
bed, but he's a sweet, sweet guy. So we sit in the car and
after a minute or so, I say, 'I'm going in. Want to come?'
Well, Anthony looks at me like I've lost my friggin' mind.
But we get out and we knock on the door. Mrs. Wegman
comes to the door. I say, 'Mrs. Wegman, I'm Susan Giles.
We've spoken on the phone.' Well, poor Mrs. Wegman is
about to pass out. I say, 'Was my husband here ten minutes
ago?' She doesn't answer me. She's trying to figure out
who in the hell Anthony is. I say, 'Mrs. Wegman, I thought
we understood each other. I thought we had an *arrangement* here. Your daughter is going at it with my husband
again, isn't she?' Two weeks later, your father stops seeing
Sherrie. I say, 'Glen, is this over?' He says, 'Oh, Susan,
Susan, it's over. I don't know what I was thinking about.'
Your father is a real bullshit artist, Jeffrey. When he was
up against a wall, he used to cry. And it was so weird — so
out of character — that I bought it every time.

"After that, things were okay for a while. We worked
some more on the house at 10 Gilbert Road. Your father
wanted to paint the house this reddish-brown color —
really gross, Jeffrey, like the bottom of a boat or some-

thing. I wanted to paint it this bright, bright blue I had seen someplace. I loved it. It looked a little like the water in a toilet bowl, but why the hell not, right? It was actually nicer than it sounds. Your father said, 'We're painting this house brown. No discussion. That clear?' 'But, Glen, it's so gross — it's like the bottom of a boat.' 'Yeah, well, it's better than a sharp stick in the eye.' Eventually, I gave in. I figured, well, things could be worse. At least he's not fucking Sherrie Wegman. At least the house won't get barnacles."

During the spring of 1971, the house on Gilbert Road was painted reddish brown. My father did most of the work himself, although my sister, Susan, was constantly trotting out with cool, damp towels and Fred Flintstone glasses filled with ginger ale. The project was completed late in May and my father — paint still speckling his back and the fine blond hairs on his chest — set a lawn chair in the driveway and stared at his handiwork until it was dark. Once night had fallen, he took a searchlight from the basement, ran an extension cord out the front door, and sank back into his chair with the bulb like a giant flashlight on his lap.

In June, we went to Hawaii for three weeks. My mother had taken on two part-time jobs — one with a proctologist, the other with a furrier — and had to stay home. Instead, we were joined by my grandparents, Sidney and Liz. I don't remember much about the trip. I remember cheap black and white TV sets bolted to chairs in the airport. I remember snorkeling in a hotel swimming pool — I was not an adventurous kid — and I remember being bored and having my father tell me, "Well, Tiger, it's better than a sharp stick in the eye."

While we were in Hawaii, my father would not let Susan or me use the camera, and he took very few photographs himself. Those he did take — and which were printed on tiny paper with rounded corners — were of flowers. Vaguely purple and blurred, the flowers were always seen from the claustrophobic distance of one or two feet. The members of our traveling party could not be found in even one. Later, when my parents had divorced and I thought back on the trip, I remembered that on the island of Kauai we had met up with a woman friend of my father's and that she had begun traveling with us. My father, it turned out, had clutched at the camera for good reason: he was afraid my sister or I might get hold of the thing and, with the haphazard innocence of children, bring back to our mother an image of a slim and smiling Sherrie Wegman.

My mother knew before we returned home. I don't know how. All I know is that she was beginning divorce proceedings even as our DC-10 was laying over in San Francisco. It was late afternoon by the time our plane landed in Syracuse. Susan and I, already drowsy from the trip and from the sun beating in on us, slept in the car on the way home. Ordinarily, our father would have taken us up in his arms and carried us into the house; in the morning, we would have awoken in our beds not remembering a thing. On this particular day, however, my father pulled into the driveway and slammed on the brakes. Susan and I snapped forward in the back seat and saw in front of us a house we recognized, but only vaguely, for it was no longer boat-bottom brown but a singular, impossibly bright, toilet-water blue.

My father, as I have said, won my mother from two different men. The second of them was Roger Marsh. My mother married Roger, who was ten years her senior, eleven months after she divorced my father. Roger was gentle and handsome — thin-faced with a long Roman nose and graying hair parted neatly and slicked down close to his skull. Roger worked for GTE Sylvania, and he wrote a skiing column for a local newspaper that ran with his photo under the headline PARK YOUR PARKA. He was a vigorous shaker-of-hands, and he had friends everywhere we went. Roger married my mother when I was eight. He was the first adult I ever called by his first name.

Surely, my father never doubted my sister's loyalty. How could Susan — already so much like our father — be taken in by this newcomer, a man who never raised his voice in public, who drove a company car, who couldn't sail a boat, and who had never fixed a thing in his life? With regard to myself, however, my father brooded constantly, and our telephone conversations were always punctuated by the question "Do you love Roger Marsh more than you love your own *father*?" My father, whom Mohawk had transferred to Boston, seemed not only remote, but awkward and insecure. I hardly knew what to say to him. Should I tell him that I loved Roger because he loved baseball, as I did? That Roger took me to the offices of the newspaper he wrote for and that a sports editor there showered me with yellowed news clippings and eight-by-ten glossies of my new favorite player, Graig Nettles? Or should I tell him the truth: of course I don't love

Roger Marsh. What I love is a house so quiet you can hear water moving through pipes and laundry falling down a straight, dark chute.

During this period, I saw my father rarely, although he occasionally invited me to accompany him on his flights. They were two-day trips, mostly — from Boston to Pittsburgh to St. Louis and back, say — and much of the time would be spent in crew lounges, where pilots smoked, ate cellophane-wrapped sandwiches, and milled around with flight kits and heavily-thumbed issues of *Yachting*. My father and I would stand at a window and stare out at the runway.

"What kind of plane is that?" he'd ask.

"A 727," I'd say.

"That one?"

"A DC-9."

"That's affirmative. And who do you know that flies DC-9s?"

"You do, Dad."

"Good man."

My father and I would sit down. I'd pull a *Sports Illustrated* out of my bag and he'd pull a *Sail* out of his. When a pilot approached us, my father would stand up, then lean over to tap me on the back. "On your feet, Tiger," he'd whisper, and I'd rise.

"Glen," the pilot would say.

"Al," my father would say. They would shake hands and my father would introduce me, lifting my arm at the elbow and guiding my hand forward. I must have been reticent about this because to this day, when he introduces me to people, my father will involuntarily start his lunge for my elbow.

33

Shortly, my father would invite the pilot to sit down. "You flying today, Glen?" the pilot would ask.

"No, Al, I just finished an Albany R.O.N.," my father would reply. "The kid and I are deadheading."

"Glen, listen: you bid next month?"

"Working on it."

"D.C.–Boston's a sweet trip."

"Hell of a trip."

"I flew it last month."

"Did you really? Beautiful."

"The Sheraton's a shithole but, Glen, it's a sweet goddamn trip."

"Al, it's a *hell* of a trip."

I have always disliked flying. The only explanation I can think of is that when you fly for free, you're never certain you'll get where you're going. The Powers That Be overbook your flight, and a few moments before takeoff, a voice comes through the cabin, saying "Would passengers Giles please come to the front of the aircraft?" Passengers Giles slink off the plane in deference to paying customers — everyone else certain that a bomb has been discovered in their luggage — and spend the five hours that remain until the next flight blinking in front of a green departure screen.

My mother recently met a man in Hong Kong while she was there on business. He must have been quite taken with her because when she left, he called the airline and had her seat upgraded to first class. Ten minutes before takeoff, my mother was sitting in second class when she heard a voice come through the cabin: "Will passenger Ceci please come to the front of the plane?" My mother, who has paid full fare since my parents' divorce, stayed put. A few minutes later, the voice came back — "Will Susan Ceci *please* come to the front of the plane?" — but my mother would not go.

In retrospect, my mother's brief marriage to Roger Marsh appears as a calm, colorless time. We listened to eight-track tapes. We bought Lucite paperweights that had coins and dollar bills trapped inside them. We watched reruns of "Family Affair." We told elephant jokes, such as, "What time is it when an elephant sits on the fence?" We ate fondue. My sister began playing piano — she'd peak a few years later with "Nadia's Theme" and "The Entertainer" — and made God's Eyes out of yarn and Popsicle sticks. I lounged around in red Toughskin jeans and went to bed after "Hogan's Heroes." I treasured the *Guinness Book* — the fattest man in the world, the tallest man in the world, this the only folklore my friends and I ever had — and *Ripley's,* of course. (Nobody has a stake driven through his skull and lives, by the way.) And, for the first time, our family began hoarding board games and toys. I lost pieces from them instantly — a habit that persisted throughout my childhood. By the time I was fifteen, I had lost Ping-Pong balls, air-hockey pucks, Nerf footballs, Lincoln Logs, the "bionic" arm from my "Six Million Dollar Man" doll, the stakes from my Nolan Ryan pitch-back, entire electric car-racing sets, and those tiny blue and pink pegs that represent babies in the board game "Life."

As for my mother, her marriage to Roger was a period of liberation, and she rekindled her childhood interest in painting. At the time, we had two prominent store-bought pictures in our living room — one of a frozen barnyard well, another of a swamp in the Everglades. After my mother had mastered still lifes to her satisfaction, she holed up in her room while my sister and I were at school, and copied the pair of them. She never mentioned the project to us. One day, in the midst of a conversation with her, I happened to glance across the living room and take in the painting of the well. I had seen it thousands of times, but suddenly it looked different to me: the grain was gone from the wooden pump; the barn seemed to lurch forward at an impossible angle. My mother and I exchanged glances, and continued our conversation. Then, one day, my sister paused in front of the Everglades painting. This copy was not so good. The original had been murky, just barely threaded with light, and the artist had impastoed it with swirling globs of paint. Bewildered, Susan crossed her arms and stared at my mother's handiwork for a few moments before turning to my mother, Roger, and me, and saying flatly, "What the fuck happened here?"

Everyone froze. Then Roger put his hand lightly on my mother's shoulder and said, "The old one was a copy."

"You know, Jeffrey, Roger was a nice guy. A sweet, sweet guy. It's a shame your father didn't leave us the hell alone. Even after he had been transferred to Boston, your father was always around 10 Gilbert Road. Because it was *his* house, you know? He might have sold his half to Roger, but it was *his* house. So what did your father do? He befriended Roger. Roger had to pave the driveway? Oh, Dad knew how to pave a driveway. Dad'd just help him out. So here I am married to Roger, and your father's doing odd jobs around the house. We're all inside having dinner and your father's circling the house on the damn

sit-down mower. I mean, looking back, it was ridiculous.
And what really pissed me off was how much everyone
liked him. Everybody loved your father, Jeffrey. Roger
liked him. Roger's *family* liked him. Roger's father actually
said to me — I'll never forget this — 'Susan, I just can't
figure out why you divorced him.' Jesus, Mary, and Joseph. Back then, everybody was impressed by pilots.

"Anyway, I don't know if you remember this, but Roger
used to golf a lot. On Saturdays, Roger used to go golfing,
and what did your father do? He came over. It was okay
with Roger, of course, because they were friends. Oh, they
were great friends, Roger and your father. So Roger's gone
and your father comes over and starts, I don't know, *raking*. I'm trying to ignore him, you know, but he's talking to
me through the friggin' screen door. He's saying, 'I'll always love you, Susan,' and 'Susan, you'll always be my wife
in the eyes of the church.' *In the eyes of the church!* You've
got to hand it to your father. He was a real bullshit artist.
He knew just what to say. I had had our marriage an-
nulled because people in my family just didn't get divorced. When I married Roger, half my family wouldn't
come to the wedding. As far as they were concerned, I was
still married to your father. Anyway, your father's raking
and going on and on, and I'm thinking, 'Fuck you and the
horse you rode in on, Glen.' But he shook me up. And
there was other stuff — I don't know, Jeff. Your father
and I, for all the other problems, had a very good *relationship*. This is awkward. Your father and I had a very good
sexual relationship. So Roger'd be golfing — Roger, by the
way, was an excellent golfer — and your father would be
saying this and that. I talked to Roger, but the problem
was that Roger was such a kind person that he refused to

believe your father was an asshole. Anyway, I felt like Roger had to say something to Glen. Well, he wouldn't do it. I finally said, 'Look, Roger, you're off golfing and my ex-husband is trying to get me into bed.' So — you remember the way Roger was — Roger says, real nice, 'But, Susan, I trust you.'

"A couple of months later, your father asked me to divorce Roger, and I did. I divorced Roger, and we all moved up to Boston. I used to tell you kids, 'I could have a million husbands — I hope to God I *don't* — I could have a million husbands, but your father will always be your father.' So we bought a house in Cohasset, and your father started flying for Allegheny. He used to say, 'Oh, Susan, we're gonna be a family again. I don't know what I was thinking about before.' All this happy horseshit, right? And it's sad, but that's really what I wanted — the rose-covered cottage. I *did* believe you married one person in your life and had children with that person, and that was it. Before we left New York, I asked Father Donovan to marry us again. Well, Father Donovan wouldn't do it. He said, 'Susan, this man has not changed.' I said, 'Oh, Father, you're wrong. You're wrong.' But your father and I waited. We said we'd get married in Cohasset, once we had settled in. You know: two, three months. We were together — what — five years? We never got married. We never even mentioned it.

"We moved to Cohasset in September. You turned ten in October. This was 'seventy-five, right? In November, your Auntie Anna got in a car accident a block from her house. It was bad. A kid hit her. I don't know if he was drunk or watching a girl, or what. Anyway, all her nerve endings were shattered. She looked fine, considering. But she couldn't talk, right? Couldn't respond, couldn't do anything. The doctors had no idea if she understood them when they talked. Well, I flew down to Florida and your Uncle Peter and me sat with her for days at a time. The doctors told us, 'Now, we don't know if she can understand us, so try and act normal.' So we're sitting in her room, holding her hand, and saying, 'Gee, Anna, those are some flowers,' you know? And 'What do you think of this blouse, Anna? Glen just bought me this.' Peter was an absolute saint. As always. Meanwhile, I'm a basket case. I'm running out of the room every ten minutes to throw up.

"Then one day, the doctors put some tubes down Anna's throat, she started bleeding internally, and she died. Looking back, I think it was their way of doing something they weren't supposed to do, you know? Anyway — I'll never forget this — your father told me he couldn't go to Auntie Anna's funeral. He hated funerals, he said. Scared to death of them. Ever since he was a kid. Come to find out, he's seeing this stewardess. Excuse me — this *flight attendant.* Her name is Kelly. She's from Ireland. I don't remember how I knew this, but I knew, somehow or other, that her father had just died in Dublin. One day, the four of us went out to buy a tarp for your father's boat. So your father's in the store making the order and you kids and I are sitting in the car. I'm bored, so I'm looking through some papers and I'm opening the glove compartment. In the glove compartment, I find your father's passport. I'm thinking, 'Susan, don't open it. You're gonna find out the son of a bitch went to that funeral in Dublin. You're better off not knowing, Susan. Don't open it.' I opened it.

"After that, I pretty much knew it was over. But it went on for years. What was I going to do? I wasn't educated.

Everything was under your father's name. My doctors had been giving me Valium because the minute you cry, you know, they throw it at you by the handfuls. You ever read that book, *I'm Dancing as Fast as I Can*? It's about a woman all screwed up on prescription drugs. I read that, I thought, 'Jesus Christ, I make this lady look like friggin' Peter Pan.' Anyway, your father and I went on. Whenever I confronted him about anything — a woman, whatever — he'd say, 'Susan, you must be sitting around too much if you've got to invent stuff like this.' Or he'd say, 'Every time I fly, I have a hundred lives in my hands and you're telling me — Blah blah blah. This, that, and the other thing. Susan, you need *help*.' You know, I can forgive your father for a lot of things. I can forgive him for fucking around. I can forgive him for his temper. But I will *never* forgive him for making me think I was crazy. Because, so help me God, Jeffrey, I started to think I was out of my mind. I mean, he's denying *everything*. He won't even take the blame for screwing around when we were in New York. He's saying, 'If you had just put an end to it when you were pregnant with Susan Karen. If you had just *made* me stop.' Honest to God, I'm like, 'Geez, I *thought* I put my foot down, but maybe I didn't.'

"When Susan was fifteen, sixteen — this you *gotta* remember, Jeffrey — she started having a lot of problems. Just like her father. She was screaming and swearing. She was violent. I had to mark the vodka decanters with lipstick so I knew how much vodka I had. People used to come over and say, 'You got lipstick all over everything.' 'Yeah, well, I got a teenage daughter, what can I tell you?' Needless to say, Susan's drinking the vodka anyway, and filling the decanter up with water. You know me, I only served Absolut. Of course, thanks to your sister, it tastes like fuckin' water. People are sitting in my living room going, 'What the hell kind of booze is this?'

"When Susan was seventeen, things started disappearing. Earrings, candlesticks. I said to your father, 'Glen, she's stealing stuff. We're gonna have to get her help.' Well, Dad just can't believe I'm saying this. He says, 'You're crazy, woman. Accusing your own *daughter*.' You know how I finally figured out she *was* stealing from me? I was collecting two-dollar bills. They were from, I don't know, the Bicentennial. One by one, the two-dollar bills start disappearing. Then one day your sister owed me some money. Overdue library books — something like that. I used to think that if I made *her* pay the fines she'd remember the next time, right? So I say, 'Susan, where's the money you owe me?' She says, 'I don't owe you any fucking money.' We have a huge go-round. Finally, she flings a fistful of bills at me. Needless to say, they're all brand-new two-dollar bills. I told your father. I said, 'Look, Glen, I'm really worried about Susan Karen.' He said, 'You're nuts. Don't waste my time.'

"Then Susan got picked up a couple of times for Minor-in-Possession. Your sister liked rum, apparently. I used to go down to the Quincy court to get her out. This went on so often that the bailiff finally said to me, 'Your daughter's gonna wind up in jail. What the hell kind of mother are you?' Well, I just couldn't take it. I started crying like you wouldn't believe. The judge looks at me. He says, real nice, 'Come here for a minute. Forget about your daughter. Your daughter's going to be all right. But I think you should get counseling. We have a woman here, her name's Joan Zahn. Please call her.' I said I would. I never did.

"Well, Joan Zahn, God bless her, called *me*. I put her off, I put her off. Then one day, your father and I were having a fight — I don't know what over — and he threw me down the stairs. I thought I was gonna have a nervous breakdown. I'm like a crazy lady crying. The phone rings and it's Joan Zahn. I'm hyperventilating. I can barely talk. She says, 'Susan, Susan, what's the matter?' I say, 'I fell down the stairs, Mrs. Zahn.' She says, 'Susan, I want you to come down here right now.' I say, 'I'm not dressed, Mrs. Zahn.' She says, 'Susan, *get* dressed.'

"Joan Zahn, God bless her, there were times when I saw her five times a week. You know, two or three hours at a time. She went on vacation, she called every day from *Texas*. And I couldn't pay for any of this. I had no money. Everything was under your father's name. We weren't married so I didn't have health insurance. Your father — after fifteen years of telling me I needed help — couldn't believe I needed help. You know? He sure as hell wasn't gonna pay for it. Only once did he even meet Joan. Your father actually had the balls to say to her, 'I'm uncomfortable in offices. Why don't I buy you a drink?' You know how your father used to do: very charming. Well, that didn't fly with Joan. She thought he was nuts. Joan didn't give a shit if he was a pilot or not. She said, 'Susan, your husband's off the damn wall.' She was the first person to ever tell me that. Finally, here was somebody who *agreed* with me. 'Susan, I don't care if your husband finds you screwing somebody from Eastern, he *cannot* hit you.'

"Joan was afraid I was gonna get addicted to drugs — you remember all those pill bottles in the cabinet with the water glasses? She took me off Valium. After that, if your father hit me, I'd call the Cohasset police. Well, what a

42

bunch of friggin' winners they are. I'd tell them what was going on — I mean, I was *petrified* of your father — and they'd say, 'Oh, we can't get involved in marital disputes.' I'd say, 'I'm not married to the bastard!' And they'd say — I'll never forget this — 'You're not *married* to him? Don't you know it's a crime in Massachusetts to live with somebody you're not married to?' Well, now I'd be ripping mad. I'd say, 'I'm getting beaten up and you're gonna arrest *me?* Well, I've heard fuckin' everything.' What I didn't know at the time was that whenever I called the police, there was an item about it in the *Cohasset Mariner,* under 'Police Log.' You know, 'Reservoir Road. Wife in hysterics.' This is a small town, and I understand that for a lot of years we entertained a lot of people.

"One time, a friend of ours said, 'Susan, you want to read a book about your husband? Read *The Great Santini.*' I said, 'Thanks, but no thanks.' I completely forgot about it. A couple of years later, after we'd split up, I went to the movies on a date. You remember Ted? Well, Ted took me to see *The Great Santini.* I thought it'd be some magic thing. What do I know, right? The lights go out and the titles come on and, all of a sudden, there are all these airplanes, all these men in uniforms. I think, 'Oh my God, *The Great Santini*!' Ten minutes into the movie, I'm hysterical crying. Ted thinks I'm totally nuts. I never saw the end of the picture.

"It was Joan Zahn who convinced me to throw your father out of the house. Well, your father wouldn't show up in court. Every time we set a court date, Allegheny would write him a note saying he had to fly a trip that day. I mean, Christ Almighty. They were as bad as Mohawk — they really took care of their own. Finally, Joan and I went to court alone and got a restraining order. Jeffrey, I was petrified. The judge starts asking me questions and I'm crying like a crazy lady. I'm hyperventilating. I can't answer the questions. Joan stands up — she worked for the Quincy courts so everybody knew her — and Joan says, 'Your Honor, I've met this man and he's off the damn wall.' God bless Joan, you know? Joan says, 'Your Honor, he's been hitting her.' Well, the judge looks at me, and he says, 'Susan, your husband is never going to hit you again.' He's sitting way up high. I'm looking up at him like a little kid. Anyway, the judge looks at me and says, 'Susan, your husband is never going to hit you again.'

"The judge issues a restraining order. It's now a felony for your father to come to the house. I call up his stewardess friend Kelly and I say, 'Do me a favor, honey, and marry the prick.' I change all the locks on the house. He calls, of course — I'm hanging up on him six, seven times a day. Jeffrey, I'm scared to death of the bastard. But I'm thinking, He'd have to be nuts to come here now. To be on the safe side, I asked your Uncle Peter to stay with us for a couple of weeks. My brother Peter — he's the sweetest man in the world. He cheered me up, you know? Just sat around with me. Eventually, your father stopped calling. Well, two days after Peter leaves, I hear this noise at the window. Jeffrey — with God as my witness — your father has climbed onto the friggin' roof and is trying to get in. I'm out-of-my-mind afraid. He's at the window, and he's saying, 'Don't call the police, Susan. Don't call the police.' Then, through the window, mind you, he starts telling me how breaking and entering is a felony, and did I want him to lose his job, and how was I gonna support you kids? Well, I stopped for a minute. And I walked over to the window and I said, 'Glen, you really got balls. Fuck you and the horse you rode in on.' Then I called the police. The Cohasset police. When they came — see, 'cause they *had* to come this time — your father was sitting cross-legged on the roof."

I I

ARE THE KENNEDYS GUN-SHY?

I F WE ARE the generation that will never be able to afford a house, what will happen to all the houses?

From the north, driving into Cohasset is a tedious business. The route is lined with Toyota dealerships, car washes, churches that have been converted into movie halls, Child Worlds, giant white Stop & Shop supermarkets that loom like lunar settlements, dry cleaners, hair salons, Polynesian restaurants in which one might order, say, a Pu Pu Platter and pork fried rice, and minimalls with names like Jonathan Livingston Seagull Square. There is nothing in particular to look at here, but because the roads are thin and winding, drivers are well advised to keep looking.

If one drives into Cohasset from the south, there are a few pretty stretches of land. At one point, the road passes a small, vaguely Japanese-looking park with stone benches and a waterfall. At another, it passes over a bridge: ten or fifteen fishing boats sit in a harbor to the right; to the left, a river dead-ends into a vast, rippling marsh.

Whenever I drive people to Cohasset for the first time, I approach the town from the south, though this involves lengthy detours. Once we've crossed the town line, I drive toward Forest Avenue. I let my companions believe that this is the only route to my mother's house, but in fact it is a circuitous one, adding time to a trip that has already consumed five or six hours.

Forest Avenue is a long, hilly road that cuts through a forest. Driving up it, one seems to be driving deep into the middle of nowhere. Then, at the top of the last hill, the trees give way, one's visibility darts ahead three miles or so, and one suddenly sees the great, flat, blue Atlantic. At the bottom of the rather steep grade is a sea wall through which countless cars have crashed and a rocky beach known as Rocky Beach. A half mile offshore is a tiny island upon which sits a shuttered-up, shingled house, formerly the summer home of John Quincy Adams or some such. I explain all this to my friends as I drive; I point out the Boston skyline, which rises to their left over a more modest skyline belonging to the town of Hull; and I turn onto Jerusalem Road.

On one side of Jerusalem Road, there is a string of immense houses, permanent and white, pointing their flagpoles toward the ocean. On the other side — the side closest to the Atlantic — the homes are less regal. To recommend this side of the street, though, there is the fact that one could leap from one's bedroom window and land in the sea. The people who own these houses are not prone to such things, of course. Still, on the stifling nights of July and August, they wake up in their beds to the sound of car doors slamming. They hear the voices of teenagers circling their houses, the incidental clanging of deck furniture, the whispering sound of shirts and jeans being stripped off, and then, from below, a short volley of splashes. Ten minutes later, they wake up again — this time to the sound of cars rushing off.

Farther down Jerusalem Road — on the wandering

route to the house I grew up in — one finds marshes and inlets and a long, sandy beach known as Sandy Beach. During the day, the beach's population is broken down like this: to the right, one sees shrieking, pink-faced kids from Cohasset High School; in the middle, creased and darkened adults known, fondly in most cases, as "townies"; and, to the left, fleshy, white out-of-towners who don't know they need a permit to park in the lot, and who will discover on their windshields a ten-dollar ticket, which they will tear in half.

On Friday and Saturday nights, Sandy Beach is exclusively the dominion of teenagers. There's not much for young people to do in Cohasset and the police tend not to harass minors about drinking. At eleven o'clock, when the beach closes for the night, the officers simply flash their lights, and everybody heads for the harbor. At eleven-thirty, the police clear out the harbor, and everybody heads for Whitney Woods, which gets cleared out at midnight.

I never drank when I was growing up, but my sister and her friends did. Even now, when I drive by Sandy Beach, I imagine my sister sitting behind the wheel of my father's forest green Ford station wagon. She is drinking, listening to the radio, and having a conversation along the lines of, "Chuckie! *Chuckie,* would ya get in the fuckin' caw!"

"Oh Susan, leave him alone."

"My dad's gonna be pissed. Chuckie! Chuckie — fuck you — get off the fuckin' hood, and get in the fuckin' caw!"

Though I didn't drink, I did spend a lot of time driving along Jerusalem Road. It was beautiful in all seasons — when storms were bad, waves folded on top of the road — and the long, out-of-the-way drive served some of the same purposes that drinking served for my sister: it kept one out of the house, it wasted a little bit of all that unprecious time.

About a mile and a half beyond Sandy Beach, Jerusalem Road arrives at the Cohasset Common. It is a long, perfect lawn, interrupted only by a Unitarian church and bordered on two sides by white, black-shuttered houses. The Common is a great photo opportunity. When I was growing up — during the heyday of the unfortunate slogan "Makin' It in Massachusetts" — photographs of the lawn seemed to be everywhere. They were on the covers of phone books, above bars in restaurants, on promotional spots for local TV, and in the dreamy, New England photograph books that sat on everyone's coffee table under a Tall Ships ashtray.

Photographs of the Common — like pictures of wrens and lighthouses and lobster boats — were meant to make New Englanders feel a part of something unspoiled and abiding, I suppose. My family moved to Cohasset from upstate New York in 1975, when I was nine. My sister and my father, both of whom love to sail and swim, took to New England eagerly. As for my mother and me — we spent years feeling displaced, feeling that everything around us was slightly unreal. To this day, Cohasset's Common looks to me like the cover of a phone book.

Just past the Common — closer still to my mother's house on Reservoir Road — one finds Cohasset's downtown district. This stretch of road is roughly a quarter of a mile long, and features, among other things, the Pilgrim Cooperative Bank, the Colonial Pharmacy, and Cohasset

Hardware. When I was young, my father used to send me down the hill to pick things up at Cohasset Hardware. He would be involved in some great, sprawling project in the basement, and he'd suddenly need a drill bit. I'd walk down Pleasant Street slowly, ripping leaves from the maple trees that stood along the road. I had no earthly idea what a drill bit was, and the idea of having to find, purchase, and deliver one filled me with an apprehension quite indistinguishable from nausea. When I reached the store, which was run by a gangly, ruddy-faced man who always wore a Boston University sweatshirt, I'd just wander down the various aisles. I'd dig my hands into buckets filled with steel washers; I'd check out the whiffle-ball bats; I'd watch the wild, vibrating machines that mixed cans of paint; and then I'd return home and tell my father that the hardware store was out of drill bits.

"And they were out of wing nuts when you went on Saturday," he'd say.

I'd pause, trying to think of an answer. "Maybe we ought to shop somewhere else, huh?"

Unless my mother was there to intervene on my behalf (which, at this late date in her relationship with my father, she would do ferociously and gladly), my father would lead me out to his station wagon and drive me back down to Cohasset Hardware. When we pulled up — the store's massive American flag snapping overhead — he'd turn off the engine, gesture in the direction of the door, and tell me, "Try again, Tiger."

"But Dad — "

"No discussion."

I'd go inside and, staring at the buckled floors, find the man in the B.U. sweatshirt and wait for him to notice me.

Once he did, I'd say, "Drill bits?" To which he'd say, "How big?" To which I'd say, "Pretty big, I think."

Cohasset's Police Department lies half a mile from the center of town. I've been in the building a couple of times — to obtain bicycle permits — but my only real impressions of the town's police force come from stories that I've heard over the years. Stories, for instance, about the time a seventeen-year-old named Ricky Barnes walked into the Police Department at two in the morning. There was only one officer on duty, and Ricky Barnes went up to the counter and told him, "I got a call saying you guys found my wallet. I came to get it." The night officer retired to a back room to look for the wallet in question, at which point Ricky Barnes hopped over the counter and — who can say why? — defecated on the floor. A moment later, he had hopped back over the counter and fled the building.

For the most part, the Cohasset police seemed occupied with dull, small-town duties. Whenever the high school track team had an "away" meet in Hull — a town with which Cohasset youths had a violent, long-standing rivalry — the police escorted our buses back and forth across town lines.

And, of course, there were petty acts of vandalism: there was, for example, a woman who lived on a channel off Rocky Beach. One day, while she was on the phone, her four-year-old daughter wandered into the water and drowned. A few months later, the woman had a life-size cement statue of her dead daughter made and set out in her backyard. I drove by the statue many times — the girl, who is barefoot, has straight, shoulder-length hair held back in a ribbon — but I could never decide if it was heartbreaking or simply macabre. In any case, every so often someone would come along in the middle of the night and chuck the statue into the channel. The next morning, the woman would fly into hysterics, and summon the police to fish it out.

The Cohasset police also spent some time taking care of their own. One officer, who was the son of a local selectman, had a habit of getting drunk and riding his motorcycle through town naked. Not much could be done about it, needless to say, and the naked cop more or less did as he pleased. Once, he got jilted by his girlfriend. He responded by getting tanked, driving to the woman's house, and shooting up her garage door. She did not bother calling the police.

I never set out to collect stories about the Cohasset police — about the goings-on in that squat brick building that sits a mile from my mother's house. Still, somehow or other, they've stuck to me. The only explanation I can think of is that, looking back, my adolescence seems to have been filled with policemen. By 1980, when I was fourteen, the police were routinely being called in to arbitrate disputes between my mother and my sister, and, while he was still living with us, between my father and my mother. The most primal fear I had as a youngster was that one day a friend and I would arrive at my house after school and find a squad car parked in the drive. My father would be off flying a trip; my mother and my sister would be shouting at each other on the lawn. This fear of mine was made worse by the fact that Cohasset seemed so traditional — "So fuckin' *married*," as my twice divorced mother often said, leaning on her elbows at the kitchen table — and that all my friends lived back down on the Common in that pristine row of white, black-shuttered houses.

My mother didn't want to live on Reservoir Road. The house she had wanted my father to buy — the house for which she lobbied constantly from the moment she saw it until five minutes before my father bent down to sign papers on what would become our Reservoir Road home — was a Spanish-style villa that overlooked Cohasset harbor. To reach it, one traveled up an impossibly steep and narrow road, which had once been covered with white stones but which was now more or less bald. The house itself had a terra-cotta roof and a circular drive, in the middle of which stood an overgrown fountain. There wasn't another house within half a mile, and the lot, untended for many years, was choked with trees.

Inside the house there was an enormous, airy living room with balconies at either end. The floors were made of wide, stained oak boards, and everything in the room had a soft, rounded look: the doorways, the windows, even the stone fireplace. On our first visit to the house, my mother, captivated, sat down on her hands and stared up at the thirty-foot ceiling. My father walked around the place knocking on things perfunctorily, then went out to sit in the car. We returned to the house several times at my mother's request, although we all knew — even the real estate agent knew, I'm sure — that my father would never buy it.

"You want me to *live* here?" he said to my mother as we drove away from the villa for the last time. "What am I, Man of La Mancha?"

"Glen, try being open-minded for once," my mother told him. "It's a gorgeous house."

"Jesus, Susan, you need a search party just to *find* the place," he said. "And that driveway! How are you going to get up that driveway in the winter? You going to ride a mule, or something?"

My mother turned and stared blankly out the window.

"All right," my father said. "Say we get the house for seventy thousand. Then we have to sink another twenty into repairing it. Twenty *easy*. Do you have that kind of money, Susan?"

"No, Glen, *you* have that kind of money."

"Not in a million years."

"Glen, I didn't leave Roger Marsh — I didn't leave New Hartford to come live in some shithole," my mother said.

My father, watching the villa recede in the rearview mirror, turned to her: "And I didn't come to live in a Taco Bell."

The plain, shingled house my parents bought on Reservoir Road has as its chief — and perhaps *only* — selling point the fact that it sits on the highest hill in Cohasset and that, on a clear day, one can gaze out the living room window at a strip of the ocean. This wasn't enough for my mother. She hated the house, and she decorated it haphazardly — a couple of disproportionately large jade plants, her old paintings of the Everglades and the barnyard well — as if one day she planned to walk out the front door without taking anything with her. As it would happen, of course, my father would leave and my mother would end up with the house.

*

For the last year that my parents lived together, they slept in different rooms. My mother could be found in the master bedroom on the second floor, my father on the third floor, across from the attic, in what was meant to be a guest room. His room was small, peach-colored, and filled with afghans and quilts. Against one wall was an armoire containing my sister's long-neglected collection of Madame Alexander dolls — Rapunzel, Scarlett O'Hara, Cinderella (before *and* after) — and, against another, a desk stacked neatly with my mother's books: *What Color Is Your Parachute?*, *Passages*, *The All Color Book of Cats*, *The Complete Poems of Elizabeth Barrett Browning*.

If the repercussions of finding one's parents in bed together are so great, what, I've often wondered, are the repercussions of *never* finding one's parents in bed together? In the evenings, my mother would sit up in her bed talking into a tape recorder. It was a cheap Sony that I had passed on to her myself. I had used it to tape records — part of a primitive system which involved simply holding the recorder up to the speaker. Unfortunately, I had been forced to abandon it because so much arguing was done in the house that, between songs, the machine picked up a good deal of shouting. For years, I listened to a Doobie Brothers tape on which one could hear — just after "Takin' It to the Streets" — my mother holler, "Jesus, Mary, and *Joseph*, Susan."

Now, my mother sat up in bed with the tape recorder, talking. Her therapist, Joan Zahn, had suggested some confidence-building tapes for her to listen to. My mother, however, had tired of them quickly, and was now taping over them with long, invective-charged monologues about my father, my sister, myself, the godawful house, and, occasionally, Presidents Ford and Carter. From my room across the hall, I could hear her rattling on at all hours. It wouldn't have bothered me if I thought my mother had been using the tape recorder to rid herself of her anger. Instead, she seemed to be using the machine to shape and sharpen it. In the morning, the four of us would sit at the breakfast table, and my mother would launch into a polished diatribe, the rough origins of which I had heard the previous night. These diatribes always began with stiff, unnatural phrases, and I instinctively froze up and stopped listening the moment I heard one: "If I may . . . ," for instance, or, "It has occurred to me of late . . ."

In the evening, while my mother was busily filling tape after tape with her strange dress rehearsals, my father was flipping through magazines and manuals. The wall behind his bed sloped at a severe angle. In order to sit up in bed and read, he had to double over and crane his neck forward. My father would attempt this for ten or twenty minutes, then fall asleep. Occasionally, my sister or I would go up to see him and find a copy of *Sail* face down on his chest, his TV illegible with static, his suitcase in disarray on the floor, as if it had burst open in the night.

Whenever my parents did wake up together — as a result of alcohol or nostalgia or lust — they would call my sister and me in for breakfast in bed. Susan would jump down on top of them, laughing, and I'd sit on the floor. I was wary of these reunions. Highs like this, I had found, led only to lows. Frankly, I preferred it when my parents ignored each other, when they behaved like strangers to each other. Still, I'd come grudgingly, nervously to their bedroom and we'd eat waffles or fried dough — my sister saying, "I love you guys *so* much," my mother saying, "Jeffrey, come sit on the bed, honey."

By dinnertime, my father would be gone. My mother, my sister, and I would be sitting at the table eating fondue — I remember wincing and sliding my chair back every time one of them dipped her fork into the boiling oil — and my mother would be saying, "It has occurred to me of late . . ."

After my mother kicked my father out of her life for the second time — after the Cohasset police came to fetch him off the roof — our house on Reservoir Road fell almost immediately into a state of disrepair. No doubt, this was partly because my mother found herself physically and emotionally exhausted. For months, she slept late and went to bed early — mounting and descending the stairs in a drugged slow motion and letting the lights burn night and day.

In a way, though, I think we actually willed the house into disrepair, hoping that it would annoy my handyman father when he came to visit. That April, a storm knocked over our TV antenna and dragged it halfway down the roof; in May, our basement flooded, setting empty boxes adrift in a pool of water. Newspapers piled up. Shingles dropped off the house. The living room windows began to leak, and the bulb in the refrigerator blew. My sister, who was sixteen at the time and who was bent on making a statement by spending all of her time with our father, wasn't around much, and my mother and I left everything the way we found it: peeling, lopsided, spent.

And then there was the grass. This was entirely my

jurisdiction and — out of anger, perhaps, but also out of an insurmountable laziness — I just let it grow. It grew until it was knee-high over the septic tank, until one could lose in its clotted depths not just a baseball but a bat. Our house happened to be near Cohasset High School, and every day kids trooped through our yard, beating down a narrow path as they went. I was fourteen at the time, and I'd sit upstairs in my bedroom watching them. One day, I imagined, the lawn would be so overgrown that it would swallow the kids up — all I'd be able to see from my window would be umbrellas and Red Sox caps floating on the tips of the grass.

Our neighbors could have lived without us. Across the street, in a severe, angular house whose architecture had once been referred to as "modern," there lived an enormously fat man who taught Spanish at Cohasset High. Every Sunday morning at nine, Mr. Lodge would appear atop his sit-down mower and cut his lawn in long, perfect strips, each of which seemed, in the morning sun, to be a different shade of green. At ten, he would emerge from his garage with a standard, hand-operated mower and, adjusting his goggles, mow under pine trees and bushes. By ten-thirty, Mr. Lodge would be doing what I thought of as detail work with a weed-whacker. This Sunday morning ritual seemed interminable — after the weed-whacker was retired, I half expected my neighbor to come out of his house bearing pinking shears and have at the lawn on his hands and knees. By eleven, however, he and his wife were ensconced in their maroon Buick and gliding down Pleasant Street to mass at St. Anthony's.

My mother disliked Mr. Lodge unreservedly. Once,

when she found me sitting on the porch watching him brandish his weed-whacker over a stubborn knot of crab grass, she sat down next to me Indian-style, folded her hands, and explained the phrase "anal retentive." Apart from his obsessiveness, my mother disliked Mr. Lodge because, like many of our neighbors, he seemed genuinely embarrassed to have a divorced woman and her children — a daughter who drank, a son who hadn't mowed the lawn once since the thaw — living across the street.

Mr. Lodge liked my father, of course. He'd liked him ever since we first moved in, and my father established his home-improvement mettle by digging up the front yard and installing a cobblestone car-park. When he came visiting, my father, who always seemed to be wearing his airline uniform now, would park his car and walk across the street to greet Mr. Lodge.

"I see you've got the weed-whacker out, Mr. Lodge," he said on one occasion.

"That I do, Captain Giles."

"Now, what does that use? Some sort of fishing line?"

"Cat gut."

"Cat gut. *Beautiful.* And it gets at those — "

"Those hard to reach places."

"Under bushes."

"It gets under bushes, yes."

"And if you need more line? Let's say the line snaps."

"You just tap it on the ground and — "

"And more line comes out. *Beautiful.*"

My mother, who knew that my father's display of neighborliness was for her benefit, watched out the kitchen window, shook her head, and said, "Everybody *loves* a fuckin' pilot." By the time my father came back across the street and knocked on our door, my mother was in her red Toyota Corolla and halfway down the street.

When my father visited us during these first few months that followed his separation from my mother, he invariably tried to restore the entire house and yard to order in a single afternoon. "Jeff, did you notice the antenna's falling off the roof?" he'd say. "I'm going to fix it. Otherwise, it's going to kill somebody, sure as you're a foot high."

If my mother was home, she'd say, "No way, Glen," and tell him that over her goddamn dead body would he fix one frigging thing. If she wasn't home, my father would leap into action, trying to reverse as much obsolescence as he could before he heard her Toyota pull back into the drive. He'd be running up the stairs with a broken waffle iron when all of a sudden he'd turn to me and say, "How am I doing, Jeff? How much time have I got?"

Already regretting that I'd let him into my mother's house and allowed him to begin another of his campaigns of renewal, I lied. I hoped my father would leave, averting a scene with my mother. "She'll be home by two," I'd say, "at the *latest*."

"Fourteen hundred," my father would say, pausing on the staircase and turning a waffle iron over in his hands. "Good. I've got *buckets* of time."

Once, my mother returned home even earlier than I had predicted and found my father mowing the front lawn. He was only half finished, and the mower sat idling as he and fat Mr. Lodge stood talking about grass.

"So you just tap it on the ground," my father was saying, "and — "

"And more line comes out."

"*Beautiful.*"

Soon, my mother pulled up, got out of the car, and bolted at my father.

"Hi, girlfriend," he called to her from a distance.

"Glen, you *son* of a bitch. Turn that mower off."

"Susan, say hello to Mr. Lodge."

"*Goodbye,* Mr. Lodge."

Mr. Lodge made his way across the street as quickly as he could. My mother shouted at my father for ten minutes, telling him that she had divorced him for a reason, that he wasn't going to wreck her life here the way he had wrecked her life with Roger Marsh, and that in thirty seconds she was calling the police.

For ten days following this episode, the lawn remained half mowed — the mower abandoned in a tall tangle of grass — until the sight of it embarrassed even me, and one Sunday morning I resolved to finish the job. It took me four hours.

Although my sister and I visited him in his Quincy apartment, my father's appearances at Reservoir Road dropped off abruptly. I never pressed him for an explanation — I enjoyed the small measure of peace that his absence made possible — but my mother maintained that he had "found himself a flight attendant." I didn't know if this was true; and, if it was true, I didn't know how my mother was taking the news. She seemed, by turns, giddy and furious. When she was furious, she would call my sister and me "Glen." There would be a lot of doors slammed, a lot of tables overturned, and a lot of fierce soliloquies that began with the words "If I may." When she was giddy, my mother would launch into a campy routine, during which she would sway her hips and say things like, "There are two exits located at the rear of the aircraft" or "Pull the mask down over your nose and mouth."

It was summer now, and I tried to stay out of the house as much as possible — filling my time with Able Seaman sailing classes, among other things. The previous summer, my best friend, Todd Burke, and I had taken the Able Seaman course and been the only ones in the class to fail. At the time, Todd and I were obsessed with baseball, and neither of us had so much as a passing interest in sailing. Todd had signed up for classes because he had nothing else to do. I had signed up partly to make my father happy — he had a twenty-six-foot sailboat named "The Tanglewood," which I always joked was too small for my tastes — and partly because, if one lived in Cohasset, one had to at least pay lip service to sailing.

This second summer of classes was much the same as the first. Todd and I did fine for a month. All that was required of us was the knotting of a few knots, and the identifying of jibs, booms, and halyards. Occasionally, an instructor would take us sailing in fat, plain boats called Widgeons, but Todd and I — both of us prone to sea-sickness — would simply lie on our backs in the hull and trail our arms in the water. By August, however, it seemed likely that we would fail Able Seaman a second time. One Saturday, the instructors towed a small fleet of Widgeons out past the breakwater rocks. They told us to raise our sails, and follow them back in. One by one, the other students did, until Todd and I — heaving tangled sails back and forth as if we were making up an enormous bed — saw the rest of the class only as white flecks bobbing farther and farther in the distance.

"This sucks the root," Todd said. He was six months older than I. (Todd and I spent a good deal of time calculating how many months older or younger we were than each other and other people we knew.)

"Big time," I said.

"I mean, something's obviously wrong with — "

"Something's gotta be wrong with these sails."

In the end, Todd and I gave up, sat on the bottom of the boat, and trailed our arms in the water. An hour and a half later, the class was over and the instructors, drinking Budweiser and listening to "Born to Run" on a boom-box, towed us grudgingly back to the dock.

As we were dragged toward land, Todd and I talked about the two tests that, just a summer earlier, had foiled our attempt to graduate from Able Seaman to Mate. The first of the tests, which would be upon us again before long, was a swimming test. For this examination, we were motored out to the center of the harbor, dumped into the water fully clothed, and told to swim the fifty yards back to the dock. I cannot begin to describe how cold and rank and sickly green the waters of the harbor had looked to me last summer, nor how impossibly distant the dock had seemed from the boat. Todd and I had completed the swimming test two full minutes after the rest of the class, then spent a quarter of an hour throwing up salt water in the clubhouse.

The other test that awaited Todd and me was the Capsize Test. Here, the instructors overturned our Widgeon, and we were expected to swim out from underneath the hull and upright it. Again, we were fully clothed. This test combined some of the nastiness of the swimming test — chiefly, the plunge into the cold harbor — with a little nastiness of its own: the off-chance that we would be, to use a little sailing terminology, knocked unconscious by a boom or suffocated by a jib. The first summer, Todd and I had been the second pair to undergo the Capsize Test, and we had managed it fairly well. Toward the end of the afternoon, however, the instructors told us that they had lost our scorecards and asked Todd and me if we'd mind running through it again. Parts of the boat were never recovered.

When sailing classes were over for the day, Todd and I would hang our life preservers over the handlebars of our bikes and ride up to his house on Norfolk Road. Todd's room could be reached by passing through the garage, which meant that we could come and go freely without running across his parents. This gave Todd's place a distinct advantage over my house. To reach *my* room, one had to pass several rather risky checkpoints: the kitchen, where my sister and her friends, fresh from Sandy Beach, often sat on the counter smoking and swinging their legs; the living room, where anything, including *guests*, might be happening; and my mother's bedroom, where my mother could often be found watching television and drinking mimosas. Even if my mother was in good spirits, one was always waylaid at her door with her endless questions and her endless observations about TV. She hadn't watched TV while she was married to my father, and now she thought that everything she saw was worthy of comment. If Todd and I made the mistake of going to my house after Able Seaman classes, one of two things happened: my mother would say, "*Goodbye,* Todd," and pull me into the house to hear yet another diatribe against my father; or she'd stop us at the door of her bedroom, where she was watching "Star Trek," and say, "Boys, boys. Have you seen this? It's about outer space."

At Todd's house, we did as we pleased. Occasionally, his mother would shout down the stairs, telling him to do this or that, but Todd would shout back, "What is this, *Russia?*" and she'd sigh and go away. Todd's room was similar to my own: baseball cards were scattered on the floor; Wacky Packages were stuck on everything ("Hawaiian Punks," "Hostage Cupcakes," etc.); and books were piled on the desk (*The Hobbit*, Ursula K. Le Guin's "Earth-Sea" trilogy, *The All Color Book of Aircraft*). Todd's room also featured a junky stereo and two twin beds, one of which wobbled when you sat on it. The beds had previously been bunk beds, and Todd and his brother had slept in them as children. One night, there had been a bed-wetting incident and one of the boys had refused to go on sleeping beneath the other. Mr. Burke had come bounding down the stairs the next morning and, in a rare flush of anger, hastily sawed the beds apart. Now, each of the four legs on Todd's bed was a different length.

The afternoon after Todd and I were towed back to the dock, we did what we always did: we played whiffle ball in the backyard, we had lunch (Mrs. Burke was revered for her two- and three-tier peanut butter and fluff sandwiches), then spent the next five or six hours blissfully embarked on an inane project. Todd had found an antique-looking baseball jersey and cap; my grandfather Sidney had given me his old mitt, which was dark brown, worn down to nothing, and scarcely bigger than a hand. That afternoon Todd and I took turns dressing up like old-time baseball players and photographing each other with a Polaroid. In Todd's backyard, there was a chain-link fence, which we pretended was center-field wall. One of us would pose as if he had snagged a ball just before it entered the bleachers — we stood on a milk crate to simulate leaping — while the other circled around with the camera.

A few hours later, Todd and I threw ourselves down on his bed, which rocked under our weight, and pored over the photos. We shuffled them. We pinned them to the wall. We traded them as if they were baseball cards.

"You want me to give you a *Todd Burke,*" Todd said, "for a crappy Jeff Giles?"

At length, he lay back in bed, bored, and said, "You better go, huh?"

"I guess, yeah."

"Is your dad home, or is he flying?" Todd asked. I hadn't told him that my parents had separated.

"He's flying," I said.

"That's *so* cool," Todd said, and the bed leapt a little when I stood to leave.

It turned out that my father *had* found himself a flight attendant. When I returned from Todd's house that evening, I was hungry and sunburnt and exhausted from having been so long in the sun. My mother was home from work — she was working as a receptionist for a local dentist — and she was in bed watching "Lost in Space." When I passed her room, she said, "Jeff."

"What?"

"Jeff."

"*What?*"

"Come take a look at this robot."

Once in my room, I drew the drapes, put a record on, and lay down on the bed. Apart from the Beatles, the music I listened to at this time was so bad that I'd prefer not to name names. Suffice to say that I have seen Barry Manilow in concert and that I once worked myself into a fury trying to convince a friend that Styx was better — *way* better — than the Who. In any case, my mother had just bought a series of classical records at Stop & Shop, and I was now engaged in the futile process of trying to educate myself. The record I put on this evening was Beethoven's "Emperor" Concerto. I listened for fifteen minutes — the sheets pushed down to the foot of the bed, the room lit only by the watery green lights of the stereo. I had the same trouble with Beethoven, it turned out, that I had had with Mahler and Mozart: one minute I'd be getting out of bed to turn it up, and the next I'd be getting out of bed to turn it down. Things went on like this until about ten o'clock, at which time I fell asleep. At ten-thirty, the phone woke me up.

"I'll get it," I shouted to my mother.

"If that's your father I want to talk to him," she shouted back. She had been fighting with him about money.

"Hello?" I said.

"Is that your father?" my mother called from her room.

"No," I said, "it's Todd."

"OK," she said. "I want to know if your father calls."

"*OK*," I told her, and then I said into the phone, "Hi, Dad."

My father and I talked for half an hour. He was calling from Logan Airport, in Boston, where he had a few hours to kill before flying a trip. I asked him where he was going, and he said Pittsburgh and then Baltimore. I hadn't seen my father for weeks, and I asked if I could go with him. Suddenly, his voice was small and distant — as if he wasn't holding the receiver close enough to his face, or as if someone was standing nearby — and he said faintly, "I wish I could take you, Tiger, but I can't."

The next time I saw my father he was married.

John Lennon used to tell this story about meeting Yoko Ono: He was visiting a show of her work at a gallery in London. All the pieces were painted white, and most of them were geared toward viewer participation. One piece that caught Lennon's attention was a tiny card with handwriting on it, which was affixed to the ceiling. The card could only be read if one stood at the top of a white stepladder positioned nearby. Lennon started to climb the ladder, telling himself that if the card said, for instance, "Sucker," he was going to climb down and breeze out of the gallery. Instead, when he reached the top, he found that the card said "Yes."

When I think of my father and of his sweet and mild marriage to a woman named Joy — life occasionally intersects with allegory — I think of John Lennon's story about the stepladder. My father had never mastered living alone. His apartment was furnished so haphazardly that one could never tell what was meant to be the living room, for instance, or the dining room. Susan and I would visit him and sort of wander around the place, never knowing where to sit down. Then, one day, my father met Joy, hurried to the top of the ladder, saw the word, and the word was "Yes."

All stepparents being created equal, it'd be pointless to give a scrupulous, detailed portrait of Joy. I'm embar-

71

rassed to say that I've never gotten to know Joy very well. I've seen her not so much as a fully drawn person, but as a few, brisk lines — somebody seen from a moving car, say, or a figure in a fashion sketch. Joy seems perfectly nice, in a flight attendant way. She is tall, thin, and English, and about ten years younger than her husband. This makes my father the third consecutive Giles to leave his wife for a younger woman. (My mother believes that this statistic forebodes a disastrous marriage for me, just as some people believed that Ronald Reagan would die in office because he had been elected in a year ending in a zero.)

Even after news of my father's wedding reached us, all was calm on Reservoir Road. I was enraged that he had gotten married — it was hard enough to convince Todd that my parents still lived together — but my mother and my sister seemed to be quietly mulling the whole thing over, considering it from different angles. Then, one day, my mother was screaming at Susan to pick the cigarette butts off the floor of the garage. In the course of the argument, she sarcastically referred to Susan as "Glen," and my sister responded by flinging a battered red dustpan and brush at my mother and said, "Fuck you, *Joy*." I had been sitting at the top of the stairs at the time, but I now fled to my room. It was not so much the clanging of the dustpan that frightened me. My sister had adopted certain of my father's disagreeable character traits the moment he moved out of the house — as if she were standing in for him, expecting him to return and pick up where he'd left off — and my mother and I were all but inured to it. What had frightened me was the word "Joy." My sister, who was already intimidatingly tall, with big, raw limbs that lashed about spasmodically when she was mad, had called my mother many, many things before (including, when she had run out of the more predictable items, epithets like "bastard" and "dick"). She had never called her "Joy." How, I wondered, would my mother take it?

Not well, of course. Here I should note that when my sister acted like my father, my mother treated her as if she *were* my father. That is, her confrontations with Susan were especially fierce because she was fighting not her daughter but the image of a man who had come at her in the days when she was young and apologetic and sluggish with Valium. Holed up in my room, my heart racing, I heard this fight as I had always heard fights: dampened a little, but not enough, by an intervening floor. I was terrified that Susan would hurt my mother, just as, when I was eight, I had been terrified that my father would. Still, I couldn't bring myself to intervene. I was every bit as scared of my sister as I had been of my father. So I hid in my room and kept turning my stereo up louder and louder. I heard Susan accuse my mother of driving our father away. I heard my mother say things like, "Sure, sure, Susan, and meanwhile he was fucking everything in a skirt — everything that walked *upright*." Eventually, my mother just started shouting, "Get out of my house. Get *out* of my house!"

When it was clear that my sister would not leave, my mother said, "I'm calling the police. I am *calling* the police." My mother went to her room, locked the door behind her, and picked up the phone. My sister went into the kitchen and got a hammer. For years following this incident, friends of mine would pause at my mother's door, run their fingers along the eight or ten divots in the wood, and ask what had happened. The marks had obviously been made with a hammer. Some of them were thumb-shaped and deep. Others, made by the hammer's claw, looked like this: - - . Friends asked about these queer hieroglyphics, but I could never, *ever* think of an explanation.

Susan stormed out of the house only moments before a squad car lit up the trees on our lawn. As my mother was letting the officers in through the front door, I was descending to the garage, where the red dustpan and brush lay on the floor, and riding off on my bike. It had been raining, so the night was cool, and the damp ground gave off a thick, musty smell. At the time, I had a black, twelve-speed Fuji and, trying to tire myself out, I put it in eighth gear and rode up and down Pleasant Street twice. When I returned to my house, the squad car was still in the drive-way, so I rode up and down Pleasant Street again, then pedaled off in the direction of Sandy Beach. I wanted to talk to Susan — to extract from her, I guess, some kind of promise that her tantrums were purely for show, that she'd never hurt our mother the way our father had. By the time I reached Sandy Beach the police had already cleared it out for the night. I rode my bike across the parking lot, slowing down every forty feet or so for a speed bump or an empty Budweiser bottle. When I reached the end, I stopped and looked out toward the ocean. It was too dark to see anything, but the sound of the waves was acute. For a moment, I could have sworn the noise was a sound effect rather than the actual hissing, gray and white sea.

By the time I got to the harbor, it too was empty. I biked a few times around the circular drive of the clubhouse, then, lifting my bike over a chain, rode it down onto the

docks. Again, there was the sound of the water, and everywhere the insistent tapping of halyards against hollow
masts. I stayed for a while, but my mind inevitably lighted
upon the Capsize Test, which I was to retake in a couple of
months. A minute later, I had lifted my bike back over the
chain and ridden off.

Whitney Woods, where my sister and her friends routinely gathered after being driven away from the harbor, is
located on the far side of Route 3A, near the giant Stop &
Shop. I rode down Sohier Street — the hill that runs per-
pendicular to 3A — and considered sailing through the
intersection, heedless of traffic. When I got to the bottom
of the hill, though, I got off my bike, and after several
panicked false starts, pushed it across 3A.

Whitney Woods was pitch black. I walked down a narrow tunnel of trees — the branches interlocking overhead
like praying hands — until I could see the red strobe of a
squad car flashing up ahead and hear, from a car radio,
the tail end of "Another Brick in the Wall" and the beginning of "Whole Lotta Love." Before long, cars filled with
teenagers began streaming toward me. I stopped at the
side of the road and watched them go by. One of them was
a pickup truck, and inside a girl was saying, "Hey,
Chuckie, stop for a second. That's Susan's brotha."

The truck pulled up next to me, momentarily stopping
the flow of the cars, and I saw my sister's friend Karin in
the passenger seat. The unorthodox spelling of her name
was of her own devising. There had been a point toward
the end of junior high when the girls in school had re-
belled against their ordinary names and reinvented them.
I suppose had it been the sixties schoolgirls would have
abandoned their names altogether. The girls of my gener-

ation, though, had simply conducted a bit of harmless cosmetic surgery, so that, in the end, the only statement they seemed to be making was that they had too much free time in study hall. Jane became "Jayne." Ellen became "Ellin." Cindy, a tough, elastic little name, became "Cindie," "Sindy," "Sindie," and even "Syndy." (Girls in my school used to refer to this last entry as the "Australian" spelling.)

Now, in the dark of Whitney Woods, Karin leaned out the passenger seat window and said, "Hey, Jeff, what the fuck you doin' here?"

"Looking for Susan," I said, noticing, with some anxiety, that Todd Burke's older brother was sitting in the back seat. "Have you seen her?"

"Oh, yeah. She took off, like, an hour ago. Her and Chrys. I don't know where they went — probably to the packie for cigarettes." Karin paused for a second, then said, "Susan's wicked bummed about your dad, huh?"

I shot a glance at Todd's brother, wondering if he'd repeat this conversation to Todd. "About my dad?" I said, hedging.

"You know, about *Joy*."

"I don't know. I guess so, yeah."

"That shit sucks," Karin said, shaking her head and emptying a beer can on the ground. "*My* stepmother? I hit her with a tennis racket. Honestly. I don't even know why. I fuckin' hate tennis."

People behind the pickup began shouting and honking, and Karin stuck her arm out the window and gave them the finger. "Jeff," she said, "throw your bike in the back and we'll run you home."

The driver of the pickup, someone I had once seen

standing in the middle of the boys' room at school and urinating on the floor, slumped onto the steering wheel and groaned. Karin knocked him on the back of the head. "Fuck you, Chuckie. This is Susan's *brotha*."

So I never found my sister, never extracted the hoped-for promise. Still, on the way home, I did get my first eyeful of Cohasset's infamous naked cop. I was sitting in the back of the pickup. I had inverted my bike — resting it on its seat and handlebars — and was spinning the back wheel with my hand and listening to the tiny clicks it made as it went around. Suddenly, as we were passing over a small bridge on Jerusalem Road, I heard a motorcycle coming the other way. A second later, the naked cop flashed by. It had been a cool, rainy night and the naked cop was actually wearing a powder-blue jersey. It was a bit of a disappointment, but that was how I first saw him: flying by in a Bob Seger shirt, naked from the waist down.

In the past, while my mother had been calling my sister Glen, my father had been calling her Susan. One would have thought that — since that is her name, after all — his sarcasm would have been lost. Still, when he thought my sister was being unreasonable or just not paying attention, all my father had to do was put a slight spin on the name, and it would be clear to everyone that he was calling his daughter by her mother's name. Conversations had gone like this:

"How much do you want this time, Susan?"

"A hundred."

"A hundred! Not in a million years. Try again, *Susan*."

"One hundred dollars. And *do not* call me that."

Now my father had been married to Joy for almost two

months, and he had shed his sarcasm. He had also shed the grim and ancient clothes we had always seen him in: the inside-out Cornell sweatshirt, the oil-soaked jeans, the laceless boat shoes. When he had a few days off from the airline, he took to wearing gray slacks, which had been hemmed a little too high, a white dress shirt, and a stiff, navy blazer. And, suddenly, my father was free and easy with money. This surprised me because I knew that he and my mother still fought about child support, and that, to her embarrassment, my mother had to rely on the pale blue checks Roger sent from New Hartford each month. (Because my parents had never remarried, Roger was obliged to pay my mother alimony; my father, ex-husband once removed, was not.) In the beginning, Roger's checks had come with short, handwritten notes entreating my mother to come back to him. Now the checks came alone, sliding idly back and forth in white business-size envelopes.

By this time, my father had begun to visit Reservoir Road again, but he never entered the house. Susan and I would hear his station wagon pull up and then two staccato honks and bits of a conversation between my father and Mr. Lodge. Susan and I would fill a jug with water, then go outside to my father's car. Occasionally, he would drive us around Cohasset, making runs up and down Jerusalem Road or endless loops around the Common. Often, though, we'd simply sit in the stifling car and perspire. My sister and I would talk — periodically peeling our T-shirts away from the dark green vinyl — and drink water from the jug. When we offered it to my father, he'd cogitate a moment, as if over some great ethical dilemma, and say, "No, but thank you, kids."

During these visits, my father would apologize for various things. He'd apologize for not being around when we were kids; for divorcing our mother; for undermining her marriage to Roger, who was "to be honest, a classy guy"; for getting back together with her; for splitting from her a second time; for not being able to bear the loneliness of living alone; and for marrying Joy.

When my father had finished, my sister and I would be silent for a moment, and then Susan would say, "Dad, I can't blame you. Ma's a bitch."

"Language, Susan."

"Sorry, Dad."

"I know you picked that habit up from me, and I apologize, but I *will not* have you using profanity around your mother."

"I'm sorry."

"Because, otherwise, I'll personally — restraining order, or no — I'll personally come here and — "

"Okay, okay."

"*Personally,* Susan. Your mother's a good woman, and she's put up with a lot."

Looking back, the bulk of my father's visits are indistinguishable from one another. Then, one day, he announced to Susan and me that — although it probably wasn't fair to our mother, who was a good woman and who had put up with a lot — he and Joy had decided to settle in Cohasset in order to be near us kids. I was instantly sick at the thought. What if Todd ran into Dad and Joy at Cumberland Farms? What if he saw them in the bleachers at one of our Little League games? He'd want to know who Joy was. What would I tell him? I'd tell him that she was my aunt. Then why did she have an English accent? And how come he'd never heard of her? She'd been given away for adoption and raised in London. It was only now — after the couple that had adopted her had met their death in a tragic ski-lift crash — that Joy had tracked down her real parents and met her true brother, my father.

Not even Todd Burke would believe this story.

I got the feeling, from the way Susan watched for my reaction to my father's news, that she'd known about his plans for some time, and I felt betrayed. My father went on to tell us that he and Joy had found a nice spot in the woods on Forest Avenue. They'd already been building for four weeks.

At this point, I had met Joy only briefly. My father now asked if I would come down some time to say hello and see how the house was coming. I could come whenever I chose — they were there until eight o'clock every night, unless it rained — and I could stay five minutes if I wanted. When my father finished talking, I noticed that Susan was still staring at me. I told my father I'd think about it, but to myself I said, I hate you for this. And I will always hate you for this.

"Good enough, Tiger," my father said, and hugged me.

The problems connected with taping an album were by no means solved when I passed my Sony tape recorder on to my mother and graduated up to an Aiwa cassette deck. The deck didn't pick up shouting, but it did pick up cracks and pops and skips, and the tiny "boom" that occurred when one closed the turntable's dust cover. (I often mused over the question of the dust cover. If I set the needle down on the record, started the tape, and then closed the cover, I had to live forever with that little deto-

nation. If, instead, I put the needle down, then immediately closed the dust cover, the first song invariably began before I had a chance to start the tape. Finally, if I
simply left the dust cover open, it slammed down of its
own accord ten minutes later, and sent the needle careening across the record.)

The real difficulty I encountered in taping records, to
be honest, was that the Aiwa cassette deck belonged to my
sister. In retrospect, I can't think why. Her entire tape
collection consisted of *Rumors, Boston, Houses of the Holy,
Dark Side of the Moon,* and something by whoever it was
that did that song "Burn, Baby, Burn (Disco Inferno)." In
any case, the basis of most of my sister's fights with my
mother was that she felt she had no privacy. To record an
album, then, I had to be in and out of my sister's room
before she had come crashing through the door — ruin-
ing my tape faster than a free-falling dust cover. If she
discovered me in her room, my sister would grab my
record off the turntable and, holding it the way one grips
a discus, fling it into the hall.

A week after my father made his announcement about
the house on Forest Avenue, I was in my sister's room
taping Todd Burke's copy of the Styx album *Grand Illusion.* I had spoken to my father only once during the week.
He called to invite me to his house again, but I said I
didn't want to go. He asked if I'd at least go on an "outing"
with him and Joy. I said I'd think about it.

While I was in my sister's room, my mother was in her
room listening to cassettes on her tape player. There had
been a time when it pleased me that my mother and
I shared an interest, that I could answer questions and
dispense advice: don't buy 120-minute tapes, for instance,

because they always end up in knots on the floor. By now, she and I had parted ways.

The news that my father was going to live in Cohasset had infuriated my mother. Instead of taping monologues, she now used the tape recorder to record fights between herself and my sister, and my sister and me. She'd hide the machine under a magazine or an apron so that it wasn't until late at night — when one heard one's own voice shouting from another room — that one realized a recent temper tantrum had been captured on tape. Apart from taping whatever arguments started up in the house, my mother used the Sony to record telephone conversations between herself and my father. They would exchange a few pleasantries. Then, pressing Record and Play, my mother would steer the dialogue straight toward child support. (A few years ago, when I began doing interviews for magazines, I called my mother to ask if she could recommend a good phone tap, and she said, "Sure, honey. Go down to the Radio Shack. They sell these little suction cups for — I don't know — two bucks.")

My sister returned home midway through the second side of *Grand Illusion*. Hearing the door slam, I decided I would fend her off until the record was over. I was sick of Susan stomping around the house, yelling and screaming, pretending she was our father. As it happened, my sister stopped at my mother's door, and asked to borrow some money. Within moments, the two of them were shouting. Susan wanted to know why her father would lend her money but her mother wouldn't. My mother told her it was because her father had more money than God and her mother worked for a fucking dentist. Susan wouldn't let the issue drop, so my mother played her a tape. From the next room, I could tell that it was a recording of my father's voice, but I couldn't make out the words. The next thing I heard was a lamp being knocked over and the thwack of my mother's headboard hitting the wall. Without thinking, I ran into the room, pulled my sister off my mother, and dragged her into the hallway. Susan looked at me, stunned, and all I could hear was the sound of our breathing as I went back to her room and collected the Styx album, which, for the past few minutes, had been skipping in its last groove.

My father and Joy took me sailing. It was a hot, blank afternoon in the middle of August. A few weeks earlier, Todd and I had taken the swimming test for the second time — we passed, thank you very much — but only two weeks remained until the Capsize Test, and I rode my Fuji down to the harbor that morning feeling nauseous on a couple of different counts. My only memory of having met Joy the first time was that I couldn't seem to talk to her. We had had a few bizarre half-conversations — the kind where one person says, "It's nice out," and the other, having heard something entirely different, replies, "No, he's sick in bed." All the while, my father bobbed his head stupidly, smiled, and said, "See, nothing to it, guys." What had really taken me off guard, though, was the fact that Joy — as if she were trying to earn points toward some stepmother badge — had talked about my mother in glowing terms. My mother had had a fairly predictable response to Joy: "Is she thin? Did he buy her an engagement ring? She's British, huh? The *slut*." Still, here was Joy tilting her head over a glass of white wine, and saying almost sadly, "Jeff, your mum's been through a lot."

I met up with my father and Joy in the parking lot of the sailing club. We exchanged a few words, and my father opened the back of the station wagon and started pulling out supplies: suntan lotion, life preservers, a radio, a tin full of Wheat Thins, the dice game Yahtzee, and bottles of Ocean Spray cranberry juice, Gallo white wine, and generic-brand seltzer ("For spritzers," Joy said. What were spritzers?). Joy and my father divided these items between themselves, then my father reached into the car and pulled out a red drawstring sail bag, which he handed to me. The bag was nylon, roughly the shape of a punching bag, and streaked with salt. I held it against my chest in a bear hug. The bag reeked of the ocean, and, for a moment, I had premonitions of myself kneeling and throwing up over the slick white side of "The Tanglewood."

My father, Joy, and I walked slowly down the docks, which lurched under our feet. Instead of carrying the sail bag, I wrapped its string around my right hand and dragged it behind me. My father and Joy, juggling boxes and bottles, said hello to everyone we passed and engaged in the sort of patter one hears from newscasters just before a commercial. As we waited for the launch, I made a joke about my father's boat. His expression was vacant for a moment, then he said, "Oh, we're not going out in 'The Tanglewood' today."

"Why not?"

"Well, you always said it was too small for your tastes."

"So?"

"So I borrowed a bigger boat."

I unwrapped the string, dropped the sail bag to the dock, and rubbed my hand. "From who?"

"Earl Bates. A friend of mine — a pilot."

A minute later, the launch arrived. As he helped Joy into it, my father turned to me and said, "It'd be better if you didn't mention this to your mother. Earl's boat, I mean."

Joy scooted forward in the launch to make room for my father. "She's been through a lot, your mum," she said.

The launch, I noted uneasily, was the size of the Widgeons we sailed in Able Seaman, and it rode low in the water. My father struck up a conversation with the man operating it. Joy dabbed some lotion onto the back of her neck. I breathed in and out with forced regularity and stared at the bottom of the boat. It seemed to have gotten even hotter out, and the spray of salt water had drenched our seat cushions, giving them a bitter smell. After five minutes, Joy said, "Ta-da." I looked up and saw the side of a tan boat with a burgundy sail cover.

"It's a Mariner," my father told me. "Thirty-eight feet. Big enough for you, Jeff?"

The launch made a wide semicircle around the Mariner and puttered toward its stern. Soon I could read the word COHASSET, which had been affixed to the boat in black block letters, as well as the word that formed an arc just above it: JOY.

Joy looked at me with a tilted head. "It's nice out," she said.

I said the only thing I could think of: "No, he's sick in bed."

"Oh, I could *kill* the slut. Would you mind — Jeff, would you mind repeating what you just told me? Let me get my tape recorder. No, wait, I've got to call Joan. I've got to call Joan Zahn. She will not *believe* this happy horseshit. I mean, I got to work for a *dentist*? I got to thumb through *Highlights* magazine forty hours a week so Joy can go friggin' *sailing*? You know what? Come to think of it, I don't even blame Joy. More power to her, right? She got what she wanted. She didn't fuck around. God bless her. But your *father*. Jeffrey, it took me fifteen years to figure this out, but your father is what's classically known as an asshole."

Tapes were made. Doors were slammed. The ominous phrase "If I may" staged a comeback. Two empty bottles of Bacardi were discovered in my sister's closet. All this, and then: nothing. For two weeks, the house on Reservoir Road was peaceful. I should have been suspicious, but I wasn't. When in the right mood, my mother could be a wonder — when I was ten or eleven, my friends had invited themselves over just to watch her. They liked my mother because she laughed, because she swore, because she took us to movies in the middle of the day and to Friendly's afterward, because she would come down the stairs wearing a hat and ask them, "Do I look ridiculous? Be honest, kids." When she was late for an appointment with her therapist, Joan Zahn, my mother would race around the house frantically collecting her shoes and bag, then come into the living room panting, and say, "Okay, a buck to whoever can find my glasses."

"A buck?" Todd Burke would say. "*Two* bucks."

"Okay, two bucks."

"You're wearing them."

I still kept my friends away from the house, but I spent more time there myself. One night, my mother, my sister, and I just sat around in the living room. Susan was heavily into collage at the time — aside from sex, drugs, and alcohol, collage must have been a parent's greatest nightmare — and the three of us sat on the floor cutting headlines and photographs out of magazines and pasting them onto a poster board. In the previous months, my sister had covered half a dozen of the boards, as well as the back of her bedroom door and the entire interior of her closet.

"How about this?" I asked Susan, holding aloft a picture of my favorite Yankee, Graig Nettles.

"I don't know if it goes, Jeff," she told me.

I looked down at the poster board. It was half covered with a pair of giant, glossy lips, a bare-chested man, a wine bottle, Robert Plant, a Lamborghini, a pack of Marlboros, the Pillsbury Doughboy, and slogans like "Too Hot to Touch," "Do It Slow," and a couple of variations on the phrase "A Good Man Is Hard to Find."

"You don't know if it *goes*?" I said.

"She's right, Jeff," my mother chimed in. "How about this, Susan?" She was holding a piece of ad copy that read, "I've Got What You Need."

"Awesome," Susan said. "Jeff, how come Ma can do this and you can't?"

During these rare, benign days, my mother, my sister, and I tended, for the first time, to the house. We couldn't fix things like my father could — my mother's TV, for instance, had been stripped of its knobs and changing the channel required a pair of pliers and a fierce grip. Still, we could beat rugs, remove dead insects from lamps, throw away newspapers, and vacuum. Vacuuming fell to me. If it rains, one can't be expected to mow the lawn. But nothing short of a power outage saves one from vacuuming. My mother would say offhandedly, "Just do the blue carpet, honey," knowing full well that nearly every room in the house had blue carpet. I'd drag the elderly gray Electrolux from the front hall closet, and set to work. I was bored out of my mind but, truthfully, I loved the immaculate house — walking on a clean shag rug was like walking barefoot on grass.

The only real reservation my mother, my sister, and I had about housework was that it necessitated going to the dump. For a couple of months, my mother had gone alone, but each time, the stooped, sunken-faced dumpmaster had, under the pretense of inspecting her dump sticker, stopped her car at the gate and asked her out. My mother, who was still livid about the fact that strangers gossiped about her separation from my father, responded by going to the dump when it was closed and plunking our trash down outside the chain-link fence.

The dumpmaster couldn't tolerate this kind of behavior. Under ordinary circumstances, he would have sifted through the trash until he had ascertained from whence it had come, and then gone and pitched it onto the family's front lawn. For my mother, the dumpmaster — he must have had a proper title but I can't remember it — made an exception. He drove his pickup over to Reservoir Road, came loping across our yard, and rapped on the door with his knuckles. My mother came to the door. The dumpmaster took off his cap, and said kindly, "Susan, you *know* we're closed on Mondays." My mother said that she had been running late, that she had had a 103 fever, that her car had been making a funny ticking noise. "I'm so sorry," she said, through the screen door. "You hate it when people dump their trash like that, don't you?"

"Hey," the dumpmaster said. "Is the Pope Catholic? Are the Kennedys gun-shy?"

"I'm so sorry."

"That's all right, Susan. I know this has been a tough year for you."

In the yardwork arena, my mother, my sister, and I were useless. My mother tried trimming the two hedges on either side of the front porch. Unfortunately, she couldn't manage to get them even, and, continuing to hack away in frustration, she left them looking stunted and pathetic. ("They look like fuckin' bonsai trees, don't they?" she said afterward.) A day later, Susan got up on a ladder to clear a rain gutter, and, hurrying because she was late for driver ed, ended up pulling it clean off the side of the house.

One Saturday morning, my mother dug weeds along the stone wall that bordered our yard, and for two days she was laid up with back pains. When she returned to finish the job later that week, she spent a few hours getting nowhere, then hurled her trowel and work gloves across the yard, and went inside. Twenty minutes went by and she came back outdoors. This time my mother was carrying a mimosa in a perspiring crystal glass. She took a few long sips from it, then set it down in the grass. She worked awhile, grew careless, and slipped and scraped her forearm with the dirty trowel. Exasperated, she threw the trowel in the grass and went out for a drive still wearing her work gloves.

My mother came home later in the afternoon with a Sears weed-whacker. For twenty minutes, my sister, my mother, and I stood in the yard just staring at the thing. It looked so sleek and modern, like a hydroplane or a

Triumph TR7, which I thought was the coolest car in the world. My mother plugged it in through a kitchen window and proceeded to weed-whack around a maple tree. I went back inside, and I could hear shrieks of laughter as my mother, holding on to the whirring machine for dear life, twitched around the front yard like a live wire. Half an hour later, she burst into the kitchen.

"It's broken," she said, out of breath. "The weed-whacker's broken."

"It can't be," I said. "You just bought it."

"Well, it's a piece of shit, Jeffrey, because the line just snapped."

My mother, my sister, and I went outside and stared at the weed-whacker.

"Any ideas?" my mother asked me.

"No," I said.

"Susan?"

"No, Ma."

"*Jesus,* but does Sears suck," my mother said, growing agitated and looking as if she might start to cry. Shaking, she put her hands on her hips, then crossed her arms, then uncrossed them again.

"Okay," she said to me, finally. "Call your father."

How long had I dreaded the Capsize Test? Two months? Three? It had never been out of my thoughts, certainly. What I remembered from my experience the previous year had been magnified absurdly, until I could no longer tell what was memory and what was invention. Eventually, the morning of the test came and Todd Burke and I rode our bikes down to the sailing club. We were the first pair chosen to take the test, and, in all honesty, it was worse than I thought it would be.

Part of the problem was that the instructors — one of whom remembered our previous performances and asked Todd and me if we wanted a cigarette or a blindfold — had difficulty capsizing our Widgeon. Todd and I sat crouched on opposite sides of the boat, gripping down hard on its fiberglass edge. The rest of the class formed a wall on the dock and watched as a rope was looped around our mast. I was vaguely aware of their murmuring, and slightly more cognizant of the fact that Todd was sitting across from me, staring vacantly, and muttering, "Holy shit, holy shit, holy shit." Suddenly, the rope was tugged and the Widgeon rocked on one side. It was a gentle tug — one that I recognized as a warning signal. Todd, however, hooted involuntarily and threw himself clear of the boat. Soon he was bobbing up and down in the water five feet away. There was some laughter from the class, and one of the instructors shouted, "Hey, Evel Knievel, back in the boat."

Todd pulled himself into the Widgeon — his jeans dripping — and told me, "This sucks the root." After a few minutes, an instructor shouted, "Ready?" There was dead silence for three seconds and then another tug came. Again the boat shot up on its side, but did not capsize. As the Widgeon settled down again, Todd, wild with adrenaline, shouted, "You didn't get me *that* time," and then he whispered it conspiratorially: "They didn't get me that time."

Over the course of the next five minutes, there would be two more false-alarm tugs. After each of them, I would be sent tumbling into Todd's lap and Todd, for the benefit of the class, would push me away and screech, "Homo!" I don't know if the instructors honestly couldn't capsize the boat — in retrospect, I tend to think they were having a little fun with us. In any case, when the next tug of the rope came — the true tug, the tug to end all tugs — Todd and I weren't prepared for it. Five minutes later, we were lying on our backs on the dock. I had a small welt over my left eye and I was holding one of Todd's sneakers.

When I returned home after Able Seaman — Todd had asked if he could come over, and I'd surprised myself by even considering it — my father was in the kitchen repairing my cassette deck. His back was hunched slightly, he was squinting, and he held a soldering iron over a maze of transistors, which were spread across the oak table like a tiny, futuristic city. Over the course of the past two weeks, my father had come back into our lives by stages. First, he had made the rounds in the yard: weed-whacking, restoring the fallen rain gutter, doing a little corrective surgery on the midget hedges. Days later, he entered the garage to change the alternator in my mother's Toyota and to restack the firewood which, having sat in a heap for a year, had begun to molder and tumble. At the end of the week, my father advanced into the family room and taped the handlebars of my Fuji. I hated seeing him around the house — I didn't trust him and I figured he was after something — but I tried to be pleasant. He'd ask how I was, and I'd say I was fine. I'd ask how Joy was, and he'd say that she was fine, that she was flying a trip just now, but that I really ought to come take a look at their house one of these days. They were going to move in soon: they'd already installed doors and toilets, and the bedroom was being wallpapered.

Today, with my father's right foot tapping on the rung of a kitchen chair, his presence in the house seemed so innocent and natural that I wondered if I had missed something. Of course, I also wondered why he had exposed the innards of my cassette deck, with which, so far as I knew, nothing whatsoever was wrong. I entered the kitchen, quietly dropping my wet life preserver onto the linoleum floor, and sat watching my father solder for a few minutes before asking him what the hell he was doing.

"*Language,* son," he said. "What's your mother been teaching you?"

My father then gave me a long and rather technical explanation of what was wrong with my cassette deck. I didn't understand a word of it. At length, I asked him nervously, "Have you ever fixed a cassette deck before?"

"A cassette deck? No."

I looked down at the floor and then up at the ceiling. "Have you ever *seen* a cassette deck before?"

At this point, my mother came into the kitchen. She was wearing a sleeveless floral dress and rubber flip-flops. For a moment, she stopped at the refrigerator, where my father had left a child-support check pinned under a ladybug magnet. My mother folded the check and slipped it into her pocket. She then came to the table, put a hand on my father's shoulder, and stared thoughtfully at the gutted cassette deck. "Jeff," she said, watching a thin plume of smoke rise from the soldering iron and trying not to laugh. "I have *nothing* to do with this."

*

Two days after my sister got her driver's license, she took me for a ride in my mother's red Toyota. My mother had been on the phone all morning arguing with Joan Zahn. Susan and I had heard the first part of the conversation: my mother had described a scene she made in the bank after a teller asked her out, then gone on to talk about how much free labor she was wringing out of our father. My mother sounded amused and self-satisfied. Before long, though, she had begun shouting at Joan —"Don't tell *me* how to live my life" — and Susan and I had taken her car keys and left.

Now, as we drove, I looked over at Susan, who was wearing an Aerosmith T-shirt, ten or fifteen silver bracelets, and a pair of stringy, cut-off Levi's. What always fascinated me about Susan was how effortlessly she swung between fury and calm. One moment she would be working my mother's door over with a hammer, and the next she'd be staring at the hammer and wondering who had handed it to her and why. These last few weeks, my sister had been sweet-tempered and submissive. One day, after the school had called and complained about some textbooks Susan had lost, my mother and I were scouring her bedroom in search of a Spanish primer and a copy of *To Kill a Mockingbird*. Susan had arrived home in the midst of our hunt — half a dozen drawers were hanging open like slack jaws, clothes were strewn everywhere — and I remember that when I saw her standing in the doorway, I tensed up and thought, Here we go. My sister, though, had simply sat down on the bed and asked what was up. A few moments later, she had pulled three books out from behind a radiator — the two we were looking for, plus a copy of *A Separate Peace* — and handed them over.

The whole exchange was perfectly pleasant. My mother looked at *A Separate Peace*, and said, "They haven't asked for this one yet."

"Oh, OK," Susan said, tossing the book back behind the radiator. "They will."

Now, on the long ribbon of Jerusalem Road that connects Sandy Beach and Rocky Beach, my sister and I drove in silence. At one point, she asked me to dig a cigarette out of her handbag. I pulled her bag from the footwell and dug through it, finding, among other things, a hairbrush, an all but empty pint of Bacardi, a bottle of Charlie perfume, a tampon, several Frito Bandito erasers, a tube of Dr. Pepper–flavored Bonne Bell Lip Smacker, and a jar of the rubber cement used for collages. At the bottom of the bag, there was a pack of Marlboros, and I pulled one out and handed it to my sister.

"What do you think of this shit with Mom and Dad?" Susan asked me, pushing in the cigarette lighter.

"What do *you* think of it?"

"I asked you first."

I shrugged, and my sister and I were silent again. When we came to Rocky Beach, Susan turned up the steep grade at the foot of Forest Avenue. I turned around and saw behind us the white, wooden sea wall — a Camaro had driven through it three weeks earlier and it still hadn't been repaired. Beyond the sea wall, I saw the beach; beyond that, the island once belonging to John Quincy Adams, or whoever. And, until the road dipped and the forest rushed upon the car from all sides, I saw the sea.

Susan didn't talk for twenty minutes. Then, as we drove by the cement, life-sized statue of the drowned girl, she said, "You want to hear something funny? Actually, this is wicked mean. That statue? Every time Chuckie gets drunk, he dumps the thing in the water."

Early in September, my father repaired a light fixture just outside the door of my mother's bedroom. Two days later, he replaced the knobs on her television set. That night — a couple of days before I'd return to school — my mother stood in front of the TV. She had spent the entire afternoon in a poorly concealed rage because Joan Zahn was refusing to take her calls. Now, she had one hand on her hip and she was turning the TV dial swiftly.

"That's how you broke it the *first* time, girlfriend," my father said, laughing. He was sitting on the bed with my sister. His head was craned forward slightly — a permanent tic caused by the year he had spent in the guest room with the sloping wall. I was sitting on the floor near the door. I wanted to believe, as everyone else seemed to, that something good would come of our being together, but I knew that nothing would. Our family's highs, as I've said, led only to lows.

"Well, you fixed it once, Glen. You can fix it again," my mother said, and continued tearing through the channels. She stopped briefly to watch a commercial for the Everything Bag, a giant purse that had hidden compartments for car keys, checkbooks, and pens, and came in tan, black, and burgundy. Eventually, she came upon "Hogan's Heroes." The show had just started — Hogan and his men were filing out of their barracks for roll call — and my mother returned to the bed and sat down next to my father Indian-style. "This is one of those war things," she said.

I rolled my eyes. "Is that right?"

96

"Yeah, the Germans are real morons, and these guys here are all prisoners of war."

"POWs," my father offered.

"That's right, POWs," my mother told me. "They've got a tunnel under the bunk bed. Jeffrey, sometimes it *amazes* me what you haven't seen."

Susan laughed, and put her head in my mother's lap. My mother — looking down at her daughter as if she had never seen her before — began stroking Susan's hair with the palm of her hand.

A week later, Susan ran out the front door wearing just jeans and a bra. She stood on the porch a moment, panting and holding her side with the confused look of someone who has just burst into an empty room. Her right arm was twitching spasmodically, and she was holding my mother's tape recorder. A few seconds elapsed, then Susan heard the screen on her second-story bedroom window fly open. She rushed down the steps and stood beneath the windowsill. My mother, whose outline could be seen lurching around the room, flung a white shirt out of the window. The shirt was carried upward for an instant and it opened — taking on a human shape — before descending, headless, onto the hedge. My sister watched the shirt fall, and when she looked up again my mother had rolled up a poster board and shot it out the window. This too opened: on one side there was a creased, buckling collage, and, on the other, the slogan WAKE AND BAKE spray-painted in purple block letters.

"You bitch," Susan shouted at my mother, as she bent to pick up the poster board and attempted to shoot it back through the window. "You *dick*."

For a moment, my mother turned away from the window and spoke to someone in the room. When she turned back again, she threw a number of things out the window in rapid succession: a hair dryer; an alarm clock on which flowers had been painted with red nail polish; a jewelry box with the word "Zoso" carved inexpertly into its mahogany top; and *A Separate Peace*. After the book had fallen to the ground, my mother leaned out the window and said, as calmly as she could, "Give me that back, Susan. That book belongs to the school."

"Eat me," Susan said and ripped the book lengthwise on her thigh.

"Animal!" my mother shouted, then turned back into the room and exchanged words with someone. My sister took the time to collect a few objects off the lawn and toss them back through the window. Then, looking down, Susan noticed the tape recorder in her fist and threw it toward the house. It missed the open window and shattered a pane of glass.

At about this time, Mr. Lodge, who had been mowing his lawn obliviously, came to the end of his backyard and, pushing down on the cool, steel handle and swinging the mower around, doubled back toward our house. Suddenly, he looked across the street for the first time and stopped the mower short. A moment later, he dropped his goggles into the grass and ran inside.

By the time a squad car pulled up, my sister's friend Karin had come out of the house and was trying to pull Susan away from the window. The hedge was covered with clothes, as was the ground beneath the window and the pine tree that stood a few feet from the house. A speaker, which my mother had ejected from the room without disconnecting it from the receiver, was hanging suspended out the window.

Two policemen got out of the squad car, one of whom was the naked cop. He walked over to Susan. "Hey, Sue," he said kindly.

"Hey, Brian," Susan said.

"Sue," the other cop said, nodding.

"Joe."

The house was silent now, and for the first time my sister became aware that she was standing in the yard in blue jeans and a bra. Karin walked over to the hedge, picked up the white shirt, and handed it to her. Susan put it on.

"What's going on here, Sue?" the naked cop asked. He was tall and pleasant-looking, but had bony shoulders so that his uniform looked as if it were swinging on a wire hanger.

My sister shrugged. She put her hands on her hips, then crossed her arms over her chest. She started to cry. "I don't know, Brian," she said, convulsing. "I don't fucking know."

Karin put her arm around my sister and drew Susan's hair out of her eyes. "It's cool, Sue," she said. "Everything's cool."

The four of them stood huddled on the lawn for a while. There was a breeze and my sister's clothes lifted themselves off the ground, then fell again, as if they had been sleeping and were trying to wake up. No one said anything. Then my mother came to my sister's window and once more started pitching things out.

"We better go inside," the naked cop said, and he and his partner headed up the cement steps.

Soon my mother's voice could be heard banging around

in the house. "You take her with you," she was yelling. "You take her with you. Do you *hear* the things she says to me? I won't have her in my house, the animal." My mother went on and on.

"I can't *believe* her," my sister said, quietly.

Karin nodded, and stooped to pick up Susan's hair dryer. "You should see my stepmother," she said.

Everything was quiet for a second, and then a few of my sister's albums came sailing out of the window. One of them, *Boston,* slipped out of its jacket and rolled across the grass. Its momentum carried it toward the road, where Todd Burke and I were standing astride our bikes, our baseball gloves dangling from the handlebars. We'd been standing there five minutes. My face was hot red and I couldn't bring myself to look at Todd. Now, as the record spun past us, Todd and I looked down at it. "It's a shitty album anyway," Todd said, just for something to say, and we watched the record roll down the hill.

My friendship with Todd began evaporating not long after the scene in the yard. Looking back, I think the fact that it happened then was mostly coincidental. Todd didn't seem particularly bothered by what he had seen. He was curious about a couple of things, of course, and one day early in October the two of us sat on his wobbling bed while I explained that my parents were divorced, and that my father had remarried and was even now building a house on Forest Avenue. I didn't mention my mother's second husband, Roger Marsh, because that seemed like too much for a person to absorb in a single afternoon. Todd asked who my father had married. "Some stewardess," I said.

"A stewardess, huh?" Todd said.

"Yeah."

"Cool. They're babes."

Soon after our conversation, though, Todd and I became interested in different things, and our friendship dissolved in the ordinary way that friendships dissolve. The last time I remember talking to him was on the telephone. He called to ask if I'd gotten my Able Seaman certificate in the mail. I said I had. He asked if I was going to take Mate next year, and I thought he was kidding so I said, "Are the Kennedys gun-shy?" Todd said, "You're taking it? Good, 'cause I don't want to take it alone." Todd actually did go on to Mate the next summer, and passed. I haven't stepped on a boat — my father's or anyone else's — in eight or nine years.

Not long ago, my mother told me about a night when my father was sleeping beside her in the house on Reservoir Road. She said she didn't know exactly when it was, but it must have been shortly before my sister ran out onto the lawn. My mother was underneath the covers and my father was on top of them. My mother was having trouble falling asleep — she and my father had had a fight and now, sitting up in bed and watching his chest rise and fall indifferently, she'd become infuriated all over again. After a few tosses and turns — difficult maneuvers as my father had pinned her down with the sheets — my mother got out of bed and went for a drive in her red Toyota. Twenty minutes later, she was entering my father's dark, unfinished house on Forest Avenue. In the kitchen, she found only plywood floors covered with lengths of pipe and wire. What was to be my father's den was filled with sawdust, a barrel-size, industrial vacuum cleaner, a pile of *World Book* encyclopedias, and a rowing machine. In the living room, there was an AM radio and a stack of slate for the fireplace.

My mother walked up the staircase, for which my father had fashioned a makeshift banister out of a pair of two-by-fours. Reaching the top, she peered into the bathroom — beige toilet, matching sink — and then into the master bedroom. This room was nearly complete, and the walls were covered with the same faint green paper as the walls of our family room. My mother stood at the dresser briefly, trying to remember why she had come. A minute later, she was swaying her hips, saying, "There are two exits located at the rear of the aircraft," and tearing at the wallpaper with both hands.

Whenever I think of this story, I think of the first time I ever saw my father's house. It was not long after he and Joy had taken me sailing, and they were still living in their apartment in Quincy. I had ridden to the house at ten o'clock one evening. I had chosen a time when my father and Joy had already left for the night, because I had no interest in spending time with them, then or ever. The driveway was exceptionally steep and rough — it reminded me of the road leading to the villa my mother had pined for years earlier — and I rode halfway down it, stopping the moment the trees fell away and the house came into view. It was just a frame at this point, and it was lit by a couple of harsh spotlights. I remember thinking that, from a distance, it looked not like something being built, but something being torn down. The house looked scavenged and picked over: a matrix of light and shadow, a great skeleton in the woods.

III

WHAT'S LEFT
BUT LEAVING?

THREE YEARS LATER, I had my own telephone line and my mother called me constantly from across the hall. This practice infuriated me. Even through two closed doors, I could hear her unamplified voice quite plainly. If I listened closely, in fact, I could hear sounds considerably more minute: the crinkle of plastic on a library book being dropped; the pop of a pill bottle being opened; the clicking, first fast, then slow, of an alarm clock being set. Still, here was my mother calling me from eight feet away. There was always a slight but perceptible delay between her across-the-hall voice and her over-the-phone voice; and, because my mother's receiver was constantly on the fritz, our conversations were often accompanied by showers of static and errant radio broadcasts. The whole routine reminded me of the days when Todd Burke and I tried to send messages like scouts. We'd shout into walkie-talkies; we'd shout down laundry chutes; we'd shout into soup cans held together by string. Those had been adventures, replete with strange and flashy new words: perimeter, rendezvous, reconnaissance (as in Todd's oft-heard transmission, "Well, Agent Giles, I think I better reconnaissance now"). My mother's late-night telephone calls, however, seemed absurd to me — an abuse of technology. They gave me the hot-in-the-face, candid-camera sensation of being watched.

What did my mother call to talk about? Nothing. *Nothing*. That was the worst of it. "Do you want a tuna sandwich, honey?" "Have you seen this 'Dynasty' crap?" "Put your dirty dishes in the hall, 'cause I'm doing them first thing." As a rule, I'd say only, "If you want to talk to me, come to my room," then slam down the phone. Occasionally, though, I'd allow my mother to drag me into one of her inane conversations. We'd talk about Joan Collins for five minutes, and then the phone line would start its inimitable crackling. My mother would ignore it for a while, then, when she couldn't stand it any longer, she'd say, "Honey, we've got a bad connection. Let me call you back." And a few seconds later she would.

I was seventeen and I couldn't stand my mother. How had it happened? If you'd asked me at the time, I would have said that I hated her because she bored me and she embarrassed me. While dining with relatives, she would put her hot palm behind my neck and discourse on the miserable state of my complexion or my hair, which grew in an admittedly odd fashion, giving me a sandy brown, Gene Wilderish afro on the top and a flat, straight ducktail in the back. I'd pinch my mother's hand until she released her grip and shut up, but minutes later she'd be reeling off some lunatic anecdote about me. She'd whip the story up to preposterous heights, then, as she approached the climax, she'd signal me with her eyes, at which point I was expected to deliver the punch line. Forget it, I'd think. I'd watch as she huffed and puffed and cranked her arms, but when she arrived at that punch line and gestured to me expectantly — as if we were a mother-son vaudeville act, or a relay team — I'd pretend I had no idea what she was talking about. (Often, I didn't.) There would be a silence at the dinner table. My mother would let out a frustrated breath and drop her shoulders.

"Tell them, Jeff," she said once. "Tell them what you said to the nurse."

"I don't remember, Mom. What did I say?"

"Oh, Jeffrey, don't play the role."

Here my mother paused to regain her momentum, and then finished the story herself. "So okay," she said. "Jeffrey falls through a plate glass door and the doctor's stitching up his arm. The nurse says, 'Don't look at the blood, Jeffrey. Wouldn't you rather look at me?' Meanwhile, the nurse is not the prettiest lady in the world, poor thing. So Jeff looks up at her and he says — what did you say? — he says, 'I'd rather look at the blood.' With God as my witness. Eight years old."

Did anyone find this funny? I suppose my mother's intention was to draw me out. But I hated being drawn out. Had I anything to say, I would have said it. I *liked* to be silent, to nod, to smile my forced, anemic smiles. I *liked* to flee the table while coffee was served. I *liked* to retire to the master bedroom and read Kurt Vonnegut atop a pile of coats. But I was constantly asked to perform. My father had married Joy, my sister had moved in with them — only I was left. My mother's sole sidekick. Her straight man.

Among relatives, all of this — from my mother's trotting out an old story to my foiling its punchline — had the air of ritual. I suppose if I *had* ever told a joke, everyone would have gaped at me. It would have thrown off the rhythm, the chemistry. Where I was concerned, there were certain givens: I looked just like my father; I sniffed my food; I did nothing but read; I never kissed my aunts and uncles; I was the only one in the entire extended family who didn't act the least bit Italian; I "played the role." Unbeknownst to anyone, I hated the role — it made me feel prissy and stuck-up — but I could never slough it off.

Among strangers, my mother's behavior was even more troubling. She was constantly sending her dinner back, cutting to the front of the line, asking for a better seat. She quarreled with repairmen, policemen, and grocers. She haggled at stores of every size and description — she haggled without mercy. I'd watch her and the salesperson go at it for a while, then I'd grow bored and walk away. If we were in Sears, I'd drift over to Televisions and stare at the immense, flickering wall of soap operas, or I'd drift over to Refrigerators and check out those great plastic hams. When I returned, my mother and the salesperson would still be engaged. At times, my mother would be in the midst of some outrageous lie. She'd be saying that she had called earlier and spoken to someone — whose name she couldn't remember, why *should* she? — who said that such-and-such was on sale. The lie was ridiculously thin, but my mother would repeat it so virulently and for so long that the salesperson would weaken with fatigue.

"I don't know," the salesperson would say.

My mother would make an exasperated, Shirley Mac-Laine face, then look at me imploringly. This was my cue to say something along the lines of, "What, are you calling my mother a liar?" I never did.

Once, leaving the mall after a particularly long go-around, my mother stopped in front of the cosmetics store. "Let's see if they've got something for your complex-ion," she said.

I looked into the brightly lit store, and saw a girl my age behind the counter. "Another time," I said.

"Jesus, are you a baby," my mother told me. "Well, I'm gonna pick up some hand cream."

My mother marched into the store, and I followed her distractedly. She picked up a bottle of hand cream, open-ing it and rubbing it over her knuckles before paying for it. I stared at the floor.

"That's one fifty-seven," the girl said.

"Here you go," my mother said, and suddenly I felt her slick palm on my neck. "And listen — Can you do any-thing about my son's face? Pimple *city.*"

Late that night, I heard my mother dialing in the next room. When my phone rang, I didn't answer.

Boredom and humiliation — a seventeen-year-old's rea-sons for hating his mother, for cringing at the sight of her paisley scarves, the sound of her clanging bracelets, the smell of her sweet, close breath. In retrospect, of course, my anger toward my mother seems considerably more complex. I hated her — for starters — because she asked me to hate my father. I *had* hated him when I was younger, but now I was bored with it. Perhaps sensing my gradual change of heart, my mother chanted the litany of my father's sins up one side of my senior year and down the other. My father, meanwhile, just mumbled his endless I'm-sorrys. Even then, it seemed a transparent device, a disingenuous bid for absolution. Still, it worked somehow. When everything else was quiet, I heard two voices: my mother's, harsh and high, and my father's, slow and apologetic. What can I say? The rhythms get to you.

There were other reasons for the ambivalence I felt toward my mother. I blamed her for my parents' divorce. In retrospect, this seems preposterous. Consider the situation, however, from a teenager's point of view. My father had his violence and his wanderings, for which I did believe he should be held accountable, but he was always returning: sitting broken-armed and sobbing in the dim, yellow light at the top of the stairs; circling 10 Gilbert Road on the sit-down mower; crawling up on the roof and begging to be let in; fixing my mother's TV. For years, my mother unlatched the screen door and took him in. Then, one day, she wouldn't have him. She drove to Forest Avenue, ripped some wallpaper off his bedroom wall, and never really spoke to him again. It was my mother, too, who sent my sister to live with my father and Joy. Those clothes that came parachuting out the window, those records, that hair dryer — they never found their way inside again. Technically speaking, then, it was my mother who had put an end to our family. And — wondering why she hadn't forgiven everyone everything as she always had — I clung to that slim, truthless fact.

Now, my mother was perpetually starting over. I suppose this bothered me more than anything else. My father's new life was born instantly and without struggle — he had a wife who wore earrings to breakfast, a thirty-eight-foot sailboat named Joy, and a freezer full of steak. My mother's new life lurched ahead gracelessly. She smoked briefly, then gave it up and began eating York peppermint patties by the bagful. She worked at a series of secretarial jobs, each of which she quit when her boss started suggesting out-of-town business trips. She tossed and turned all night, or read from randomly selected, three-foot-high stacks of library books. She took back her maiden name. She bemoaned her stalled love life.

I found all this to be a sad, pathetic business, and I resented having to bear witness to it. My mother's lows were profoundly low. There were days when I knocked on her hammer-beaten bedroom door and she wouldn't answer for hours at a time. My mother's highs, however, seemed hollow and forced. The purposeless lies, the frequent profanity, even the aborted, mother-son vaudeville act — everything she did was for show. My mother didn't want anyone to take pity on her, so everyone did. Except for me. I foiled her punch lines. I didn't answer my phone.

Meanwhile, my father slept. He could sleep anywhere. I'd run into B. Dalton's, and when I came out my father's forehead would be sweating against the steering wheel. I'd come out of 7-Eleven and his head would be tilted back, his Adam's apple would be jutting forward, and he'd be snoring. Whenever I woke my father, he'd go through the same routine. He'd shudder briefly, rub his face with both hands, and say in disbelief, "Did I fall asleep? Sorry, son." Fifteen minutes later, I'd come out of Radio Shack and he'd be sprawled full-length across the front seat.

Even though he was living on Forest Avenue, I saw my father infrequently — maybe once or twice a month. I've said that I preferred his apologizing to my mother's railing, but, truthfully, I was sick to death of it as well. Now, when my father lapsed into his forgive-me routine, I'd just tune him out. I'd imagine I was watching one of those schmaltzy K-Tel ads: An announcer would tell us that my father had sold more records than the Beatles (in Canada). Then, my father, who'd be wearing his airline uniform and sitting on a stool, would start snapping his fingers and singing from "All My Best Apologies." As he sang — in my mind, I gave my father Tony Bennett's voice — famous titles would scroll by on the screen: "I Tried," "Blame Me (Don't Blame Your Mother)," "I Should Have Been There (When You Two Were Kids)."

To be fair, my father did more than just apologize. He was incredibly kind and solicitous. Should he roll up his window? Should he change the station? Should he get me another Coke? Then, as I've mentioned, there were the shopping sprees. While my father slept in the station wagon, I'd load up with Kurt Vonnegut books, Peter Gabriel tapes, and Big Gulps. I knew my father was trying to buy my sympathy, and I felt it was the least he could do. On a few occasions, it got out of hand. One Friday in 1982, during my senior year in high school, I skipped classes and my father and I flew to Buffalo to see a Genesis concert. (Sometimes I wonder how I can begrudge anything to a man who, at forty-seven, was forced to watch Phil Collins mug for two hours.) A few months later, I was near tears because of the typos on my Princeton application. I called my father and an hour and a half later — I wish I were making this up — we were flying to New Jersey to get another one. (In the end, I screwed up the second application so badly that I sent the first one.)

For all my father's overtures, the time I spent with him was awkward — principally because we had nothing to say to each other. My mother insisted I was just like my father: I had his sarcasm and his squint. I thought I was King Farouk. I was a real bullshit artist. When my father and I were sitting across a table from each other, though, we seemed to be nothing alike. I'd ask him perfunctory questions about his airline, his boat, and the house on Forest Avenue, which, impossible as it seems, was still unfinished. He'd ask me how my grades were, what music I was listening to, what I was reading, and what I was writing.

At seventeen, I could have gone on for hours about music or writing, but, when invited to by my father, I couldn't get out more than a few sentences. Where my writing was concerned, we had a bumpy history. One winter, when I was thirteen, I had heard that the *Cohasset Mariner* was having a poetry contest and I instantly sent off my latest opus: an account, in rhymed couplets, of a deranged court jester on a killing spree. What I didn't know at the time was that the contest was, in fact, a *Christmas* poetry contest. Before long, I received a letter from the editors with one or two kind words about my poem and several hundred more about the meaning of Christmas. This was embarrassing enough. More embarrassing, though, was the fact that the editors gave my poem an honorable mention and printed it. One morning before Christmas, my father opened the paper and there, amid all the verse about eggnog and sleighbells and Grandma's gingham apron, was my poem about the deranged court jester. It was called "Blood and Snow," or something along those lines. My father read my poem, then closed the paper, and stared at me. After that, we didn't talk about poetry for ages.

Four years later, my father still couldn't make head or tail of my writing. Like my mother and my sister, he had always made his points by shouting and kicking over furniture in the kitchen. He had, in fact, begun the war of escalation that had occupied the three of them for years: when my mother had become inured to profanity, he took to punching through walls. When even that failed to get her attention, he graduated to another level of violence. I know that some consider all this the purest, most honest form of communication — far better than the sarcasm, escapism, and repression that I resorted to. Still, it was beyond me. I hadn't inherited whatever gene it was that allowed my father, my mother, and my sister to throw their singular tantrums. Whenever I got angry and wanted to destroy something, I'd look around my room frantically. Before long, the Voice of Reason would go off in my head. The Voice of Reason said, "That Pink Floyd poster cost you six bucks" or "If you hit that wall, you could break your hand." The end result was that I couldn't go toe to toe with anyone in my family — particularly not my father. Any residual anger I felt toward him, I had to express, crudely, in my writing. Most of the time, this anger was great, blank, and undifferentiated. Once in a while, it appeared as a string of unaskable questions: What the hell had my father been thinking all those years? Did he really regret *anything*? Why was everything so easy for him now? Why was another woman enjoying the calm, simple years that my mother had earned? Why didn't I love my mother? Why didn't I hate my father?

All these questions — buried in a muck of adolescent prose — went unnoticed. My father would read a story I'd written about a disaffected housewife and her malevolent, astronaut husband, and he'd ask only where I had picked up the words "disaffected" and "malevolent." Then he'd hand the story back to me and say, "Good job, Tiger." The routine was a frustrating one. I was trying to send messages but my father wasn't receiving.

I saw my sister even less than I saw my father. She had graduated by now, and was going to hairdressers' school. Once I ran into her at my father's house and we had a fairly typical exchange. She was sitting at the kitchen table with a Styrofoam mannequin's head and all manner of scissors, combs, rollers, and wigs. I said, "Hey, Sue," and she said, "Hey, Jeff. Let me cut your hair." I looked at the mannequin's head. There was a wide gash across its forehead and an inch-long scar down its neck. "Yeah, *right,*" I said.

"Come on, Jeff. Don't be a dweeb."

"I haven't eaten today, Sue. I don't know if I could stand the blood loss."

"Oh, you're wicked funny."

Soon, my father walked in and my sister asked him to intervene on her behalf. My father looked at the mannequin, and then he looked at me and said, "Have you eaten today?"

"Oh, you're both wicked funny. I can't do anything for you anyway, Jeff. You look like fuckin' Willy Wonka."

"*Language,* Susan," I said.

My father laughed. To me he said, "Thank you, Jeff." Then, to my sister: "He *does,* doesn't he?"

When I think of my sister at nineteen, I think of a photograph of her that sits on my mother's dresser. It's one of those soft-focus portraits — taken at Sears or K-mart, probably — for which one's mother spends twenty minutes selecting backgrounds: a sunset, a blue sky, a forest. In it, my sister, who's wearing a heart-shaped pendant and sporting a modified Dorothy Hamill hairdo, leans on a fake fence post. Her cheek is resting on her hand, and she is staring thoughtfully into space. Behind her is a blurry spray of fall foliage. I don't remember when the photograph was taken, but no doubt there are dozens of copies in existence: eight by tens, five by sevens, whole uncut sheets of wallet-size prints. What I love about the picture is the sheer absurdity of it: Susan caught in a moment of repose, Susan on a nature walk. The photo bears no relation to the blur of motion that was my sister's adolescence. It is like the five-foot barre attached to a wall in the family room on Reservoir Road. My father had put it up in the days when an eleven-year-old Susan took dance classes, and dashed around the house in pink tights and pointe shoes. Now, the barre seemed to belong not just to another time but to another family.

For me, the photographs that best reflect my sister are those wonderfully cheesy ones where the subject appears three times, looking in three different directions. In the large, central pose, Susan smiles widely, revealing an uneven row of teeth. (At thirteen, she had attempted to pull her own braces off and done so much damage that the orthodontist had been forced to remove them.) In another, she has a somber expression. In the third, she looks heavenward and her face is washed with an angelic light. By the time she was nineteen, my sister had been exposed to the sobering forces of graduation and unemployment. She was still unpredictable, though; one never knew what face she'd show next. Susan had blamed our mother for driving our father away far more stridently than I, and she must have supposed that living on Forest Avenue would be

116

idyllic. In her first few months there, she may have even seen Joy as the prim, conventional mother she had never had. Before long, though, Susan grew jealous of Joy and the twilight romance Joy was carrying on with our father. Susan began defying Joy at every turn. She ran through the house slamming doors, waving her hands in the air, and shouting her dearest slogan, "*Oh* my God! *Oh* my God!" I wonder if even then Joy had any idea what she had gotten herself into.

I rarely ran into my sister at night because my friends and I didn't drink, and we avoided the places that Susan had long frequented: Sandy Beach, the Harbor, Whitney Woods. Whenever we *did* come across each other in a social situation, there was always some awkwardness in the fact that we were so radically different. Years earlier — riding my Fuji around Cohasset with Todd Burke — I had been a generic little brother. No one knew how I'd turn out. Then, by sixteen or so, I had begun to emerge: I liked to read; I had a digital watch; I wore sweaters and Dock-Siders; I played French horn in the high school band. During that period, my sister's friends were horrified by the sight of me. They used to offer to beat me up in the hopes of toughening me up a little. Often, they'd punch my arm a couple of times, and I'd say, "Oh, that's *really* sophisticated," and my friends would groan in embarrassment. Eventually, my sister would walk up, and threaten to kick the shit out of whoever was pestering me. My persecutor would back off immediately, and my friends and I would bolt.

My teachers and friends, of course, had been horrified by the sight of my sister. Susan had played flute in the high school band for a year — her flute belongs with her pointe shoes in our annals of the strange but true — and, upon meeting me, the band director asked if I was Susan Giles's brother. I said that I was. The band director, who was standing up on a podium, looked me over and then handed down some sheet music, saying only, "My condolences." In retrospect, I wish I had had the wherewithal to say "Screw you" or "Sit on it," or whatever we said in 1979. But I comfort myself with the knowledge that Susan must have made his life hell while she had the chance.

Now, by the winter of 1982, my senior year, Susan's friends left me alone, but there was still that awkwardness and the occasional "Sue, I can't *believe* yaw his sista." I was only too happy to avoid Whitney Woods. My friends and I had better things to do.

We didn't, really. At the time, my two best friends were Alan Sutton and Joe Whittle (also known as "Witless"). Alan had moved to Cohasset during the ninth grade, and we had been thrown together for an unmemorable oral report about the Trojan War. Joe had lived in Cohasset his whole life, but I had never met him because he had long hair and wore a jean jacket. (The entire school was convinced Joe was a stoner, but, like Alan and me, he had never smoked a joint.) In tenth grade, Joe and I ended up in the same music class — I played guitar and he played drums — and then spent the better part of high school trying to form a band.

Although he was eighteen, Alan hadn't been kissed yet and, as a result, he was a head-case. Joe and I used to sit around in Alan's overheated, sickly-sweet-smelling bedroom as Alan went on and on about the charms of our classmate Kimberly Douglas, or ignored us completely, preferring to reread the Benjy section of *The Sound and the Fury* and bang his forehead against the bedroom door. Alan was an aspiring writer and his room was filled with wonders: books of poetry by E. E. Cummings and Dylan Thomas; albums by Robert Fripp and Brian Eno; obscure musical instruments; Russian hats; finely carved knives; and a bamboo Kendo stick, which was intended for the martial arts but which Alan routinely beat against his forehead.

"Doesn't that hurt, big guy?" Joe would ask.

"Yes, it *does* hurt," Alan would tell him, and then start up again.

Joe was thin, with fine blond hair, crooked teeth, and a character actor's good looks. He was perpetually broke, he was a dreadful student, and, like me, he had a sadly skimpy romantic résumé. Nevertheless, Joe had a generous self-image. If you called his house, he'd say, "I'm sorry, Mr. Whittle is in the tub with the Go Go's. This is his male secretary, how can I help you?" Joe was often seen at mirrors, running his hand through his hair and saying, with genuine wonder, "This shirt looks fucking great on me" or "My *God* I'm a stud." Occasionally, he'd raise a hand, as if to silence a cheering crowd, and say only, "Thank you. Thank you very much."

Because Joe was not overly fond of his parents, the only time we went to his house was to jam. We'd breeze through the living room — rushing past his mother and father without saying hello — then climb the steep stairs to Joe's bedroom. We must have run this gauntlet a thousand times over the years, but for the life of me I couldn't describe that living room, or even what Joe's parents

looked like. As for Joe's bedroom, it was something like
my sister's room at my father's house: the walls were covered with nylon Led Zeppelin banners and headlines
about demonically possessed dolls and eighty-pound
babies. The floor was covered with half-full glasses of
milk, piles of underwear, and textbooks that had never
been cracked. In one corner of the room, there was Joe's
drum set and my electric guitar.

Joe and I could only play three songs: "Spanish Bombs,"
by the Clash; "Same Old Song and Dance," by Aerosmith;
and "Pearl Necklace," by ZZ Top. We played them over
and over again. Alan used to sit on Joe's bed, listening and
bobbing his head. When Joe and I had finished "Spanish
Bombs" and "Same Old Song and Dance," Alan would say,
"Hey, do you guys know 'Pearl Necklace'?" Then, when we
had finished "Pearl Necklace," Alan would say, "Hey, do
you guys know 'Spanish Bombs'?" As often as we played
our three songs, Joe and I never quite got them right.
Usually, we'd play for a minute or two, before arriving at a
difficult passage. At that point, I'd say, "Drum solo," and
Joe — his hair swinging in every direction — would bang
away until Alan and I forced him to stop. Joe would then
leap up, raise his fists in victory, and shout, "I'm *awesome!*"

As our senior year progressed, our circle of friends
widened somewhat. On an average night, we'd spend an
hour driving around picking everybody up, half an hour
talking about how Cohasset sucked, and then another
hour driving everybody home. Still, we were never de-
terred. The smallest excuse to get out of the house was
leapt at by all. Charles had to pick up some chicken
breasts for his mom? We'd go. Joe was going to cash in
some bottles? Okay. Jay was out of chewing tobacco? Pick

us up in five minutes. We would *always* go along for the ride. Once seven of us went to Friendly's and it was only when the waitress came to take our orders that we discovered only our friend Maureen was hungry.

I loved the fact that my friends wanted to get out of their houses as much as I wanted to get out of mine. (Charles was a notable exception: his mother's apron strings were like an octopus's tentacles.) For years, I had felt the need to feign normality where my family was concerned, but no longer. My friends and I fled from "family time" — we fled without apology.

On Christmas morning, I awoke to the sound of our snowblower. I went into Susan's old room, which was now a shabbily furnished guest room, and looked down on the driveway. My mother was attempting to clear a path from the garage to the street. She was wearing one of my ancient, pom-pommed Los Angeles Rams hats, purple boots that she'd lined with Wonder Bread bags, and a parka, beneath which extended a flannel nightgown. The driveway was steep and, owing to a surface coating that had been applied by the house's previous owners, quite slick. My mother would push the snowblower two feet or so, and it would slide backward three.

I sat down on the bed to watch. My mother seemed to be getting the hang of it. At one point, she charged ahead a good ten feet before the machine started its backward slide. My mother tried to stand her ground, but her boots gave way. She jumped clumsily to one side, and the snowblower went charging down the driveway, executing a complete turn before coming to rest near the garage door. The engine sputtered to a halt. My mother stood over it for a moment, throwing switches. She pulled the cord, but couldn't get it started. She took a bag of York peppermint patties out of her parka and slumped down in the snow.

I continued to watch my mother for a minute or two, then stood and knocked on the window. She looked up. I mouthed, "The choke, Mom. The *choke*." She looked confused. She threw her hands up. A moment later, Mr. Lodge, wearing an enormous Ragg sweater and a ski hat similar in style to my mother's, came traipsing down the drive. He and my mother had a brief conversation, which I could not hear. Mr. Lodge asked my mother something, and my mother turned — her blue and yellow pom-pom bobbing — and pointed up at me. Mr. Lodge looked at me briefly. He shook his head, causing his own, larger pom-pom to shimmy to and fro. He turned back to my mother.

Guilt-ridden, I returned to my room and got dressed. After I had cleared the driveway, I pushed the snowblower around to the front of the house and began plowing the cobblestone car-park where my '72 Pinto was lost in an enormous drift. The car was a dull, unappealing orange more or less the color of French dressing. It had previously belonged to Joy. For years, the Pinto had had a British flag bumper sticker, but days after I drove it to Reservoir Road for the first time, my mother went outside in her nightgown-and-parka ensemble and stripped it off with a razor blade. Nowadays, the Pinto was falling apart. The hand brake didn't work. The right directional didn't work. There were tiny ponds of ice in the rear footwells, in which a number of Twix wrappers had been trapped. The car burned oil at an appalling rate. When it idled, it shuddered violently and produced a bizarre chortle.

Once I had unearthed the Pinto, I shut myself inside. Snow still coated the windshield and the windows, so the car was dark and quiet as a tomb. I turned on the radio, and — flipping past a station that was doing a countdown of the Top 500 rock songs of all time, of which "Stairway to Heaven" would doubtless be Number 1 — found "Every Little Thing She Does Is Magic," by the Police. I let it play, although I figured that I'd probably hit upon a "lite rock" station, and that I'd have to start flipping again in a minute. I sat back in the seat and thought about the night before, when my mother and I had had our annual fight about Christmas dinner.

"I invited Lonnie," she had said.

"Why?"

"Because, *Jeffrey,* she has nowhere to go for Christmas. She gets lonely."

"Mom, she's Jewish. What makes you think she gets lonely on Christmas? Do you get lonely on the Chinese New Year?"

"Why do you have to be a jerk, Jeffrey?"

"Who else did you invite?"

"The Thompsons."

"Who are the Thompsons?"

"Well, there's Janet, who I met at Dr. Taylor's office, and her husband, Stewart. Then there's her parents, Kip and Sarah, who I haven't met. Sarah's a hypnotist — I thought that would be fun. I also invited Janet's brother, Fred, who's some kind of chess champion."

"Oh, for God's sake."

"Look, they've had a hard time, OK?"

"They've 'had a hard time'? Jesus Christ, why don't you invite the *Nixons?*"

"Don't you swear at me. Anyway, what do you give a shit *who* I invite, Jeffrey?"

"I just don't know why every Christmas this place turns into a halfway house."

"I can't believe I raised such a selfish s.o.b. Who would you *like* me to invite?"

"How about just you, me, Susan and Mike?" Mike was Susan's boyfriend.

"I tried having just you guys. In 1981. What happens? You run off with your friends before the coffee's even *cold*. Susan and Mike run off to Joy's house. And I end up alone. I'm forty-five years old and I spend Christmas watching *Planet of the Apes*. Well, forget *that*, mister."

Now, sitting in the Pinto, I ran the argument over in my head and felt guilty about it. Conversations with my mother always followed the same pattern. She'd say something that set me off, and I'd start in with sarcasm. My mother would tell me I was acting like a jerk and I'd know she was right — by now, the arguments were so routine and demanded so little of my attention that I could step outside myself, like a patient having a near-death experience, and look on objectively. Still, I couldn't bring myself to reverse the flow of the conversation, to admit that I was wrong. It was as if the fight had been preordained, and I had to follow the script through to the end.

What was it about my mother's Christmas dinners that set me off? The answer seemed fairly simple: inviting strangers to what was meant to be a private ceremony seemed too bald an admission of our family's disintegration. Why should anybody else know that my mother, my sister, and I could hardly stand to sit at a table together? Why should they know that even on Christmas — *espe-*

cially on Christmas — we were either bickering or bored, that we were wolfing down our dinners and hoping the phone would ring? Of course, my mother was right: I ran off, Susan ran off. It would have been foolish to pretend otherwise. But while I hated to feign normality and while I saw my recent disavowal of it as nothing less than a rite of passage, there continued to be a part of me that still longed for it. I decided that — for this Christmas at least — I would stay with my mother all day and all night.

That issue resolved, I looked across the street at Mr. Lodge's driveway. It was dry and black, and lined on both sides by hard, squared-off walls of snow. One shovel had been plunged into the drift a few feet from the front door. Had Mr. Lodge done all this himself? With a *shovel?* Mr. Lodge had been nice to my mother over the past couple of years, so I was no longer resentful of his yard-maintenance genius. Instead, I just gaped at his handi-work. When my mind came back to the radio, it was playing "Just the Way You Are." I screeched, shut it off, and ran into the house.

Twenty minutes after dinner with my mother, Susan, Mike, Lonnie, Janet, Kip, Stewart, Sarah the hypnotist, and Fred the All–Rhode Island Chess Champion, I picked up Alan and Joe and the three of us sat in the deserted high school parking lot.

"This car blows, Jeff," Joe said. He was in the back seat, stamping his feet on an iced-over footwell and drumming the solo from "In the Air Tonight" on Alan's headrest.

"It's better than the Bug, Witless," I said.

"Oh, *dude!* The Bug rules."

"What do you think, Alan?" Alan had spent the

previous night parked at the end of Kimberly Douglas's street, hoping he'd catch a glimpse of her driving by. He now had the *Collected Yeats* face down on his lap, and he was banging his head against the dashboard.

"The Bug sucks . . ." Alan said, stopping for a moment.

"Oh, *dude!* Harsh call."

". . . and the Pinto sucks." Alan resumed hitting his head.

"Look, stop that, Alan," I said. "You're gonna give yourself a concussion."

"I should be so lucky," Alan said.

"Stop it. You're gonna crack the vinyl."

"Jeff, you can go *skating* in the back seat, and I'm gonna crack the vinyl?"

Alan shook his head, and started fishing through the glove compartment for cassettes. After a moment, he had selected one and was ripping the tape out by the handful.

"What is with you?" I asked him.

"Relax," Alan said. "It's Elton John."

"Wait. What album?"

"*Greatest Hits.*"

"One or Two?"

"Two."

"Okay."

At this point, Joe leaned forward to look in the rearview mirror and run his hand through his hair. Alan, meanwhile, was busy winding the Elton John tape around his neck.

"So, anyway," Joe said, as he adjusted his part, "I'm gonna cash in some bottles tomorrow morning."

"What time?" I asked.

"Ten. Ten-thirty."

"Okay," I said, "call me before you go."

"Want to come, Alan?" Joe asked.

Alan let out a strangled wheeze. The tape was wound tightly up and down his neck. His face was a bright, pinkish red; his eyes were watering. Alan looked frantically at Joe and me, and then slumped forward in his seat.

"Alan, get the fuck out of my car," I said.

"Thank you," Joe said, still staring into the rearview mirror. "Thank you very much."

That night, I went to my father's. There were five cars in the driveway. Three of them, each of which was over ten years old and made the same chortling sound as my Pinto, constituted my father's commitment to American automobile manufacturers: a red Dodge Dart, a dull gold Cadillac about the size of a parade float, and the Ford station wagon. It was absurd that my father had three junky cars instead of a single decent one, but he doted over them sentimentally and, where negotiations with my mother were concerned, they substantiated his protracted cry of poverty. Parked next to my father's fleet were Joy's brand-new Plymouth and a Honda station wagon that belonged to my sister's boyfriend, Mike. I liked Mike a lot, and, because Mike built houses for a living, my father liked him too. Mike was shortish and round, and looked, I thought, a little like John Belushi. He was generally quite withdrawn around my family — seeing him next to my chattering sister was a continual study in the mysteries of love.

I parked my car and walked down the driveway. The outside of my father's house was more or less complete: it was boxy and brown, with three bubble-shaped skylights and a long wrap-around porch. Inside, though, a few of the rooms still had splintering plywood floors, and many of the ceilings were a maze of wire, piping, and two-by-fours. My father had long since fired the last of the contractors, insisting on finishing the house himself. And he *was* finishing it, but slowly. He'd work on it for a couple of days, and then he'd be called away to fly a week-long trip. When he returned, he'd work a little more, and then get called away again. And on and on. Joy, I knew, was unhappy about living in an unfinished home.

I entered the house through the kitchen. The floor was spread with newspapers upon which were clumps of hair, some of it curly and brown, some of it straight and gray. A few moments later, I found Susan sitting alone in the living room. She had changed since dinner and was wearing a white turtleneck, the collar of which was stained with makeup, and blue jeans. Her hair was whitish blond and cut so short that it stood up in spikes, Laurie Anderson–style. Susan got up and hugged me, and I saw that she had been crying.

"That was some dinner, huh?" she said.

"It gets worse every year," I said.

"That hypnotist chick? And that chess guy? Who *was* that guy?"

"I don't know. Mom probably met him in a checkout line."

"After you took off, me and Ma got shit-faced. We were asking that guy all about chess. He plays *five hours* a day. I'm sitting there going, 'Whatever you're into.' But he turned out to be a really good guy. Ma invited everybody back."

"Great," I said. I looked around the room, which was strewn with wrapping paper and boxes. "Where is everyone?"

"Don't even ask."

"You cut everybody's hair?"

"Not Joy's hair. God forbid I touch Joy's precious hair."

"So just Dad's and Mike's?"

"Yeah. They're upstairs washing it. I'm like, 'It'll fucking grow out.' "

Shortly, Joy came down the stairs, said hello, and, ignoring Susan entirely, engaged me in some small talk. There was something about Joy that always put me on edge. She was usually so busy killing everybody with kindness that one could never tell what she was thinking. My father — in defending his wife's mettle — used to say, "She's a tough broad. You push her sometime. You'll see." I didn't know what constituted "pushing" Joy, and I didn't want to find out. Even when she was angry, Joy never let on. Her anger just hung in the air, unspoken.

Before long, my father and Mike came down the stairs laughing. Their hair was wet and they had matching yellow towels draped around their necks. My father rubbed his closely shorn scalp and joked to Joy that he couldn't leave the house looking like this and did she know any restaurants that delivered. Joy whispered that tomorrow they'd go and get his hair fixed. Susan started to cry.

"I'll go fix us some drinks," Joy said.

"*Once* a stewardess . . ." Susan said, watching her go.

The last thing my mother wanted was to run into the Slut. Chance meetings seemed inevitable in a town as small as Cohasset — I remembered being terrified that Todd

Burke would come across Joy somewhere — but my mother had a simple plan: she'd avoid any place the Slut had ever been seen. For the most part, the plan worked. My mother had a network of friends who reported Joy sightings the way others reported sightings of the Virgin Mary or Bigfoot. Connie Collins had seen Joy buying a driftwood sculpture at the Kit & Kaboodle? Mom would boycott the place. Ellen Fox had seen Joy at St. Anthony's? Ditto — Mom hated the priest's reactionary sermons anyway. Leah O'Brien had seen Joy eating lobster at the Red Lion Inn? This one hurt — my mother lived for lobster. Still, what was she, a cripple? She could cook her own.

Whenever I returned from my father's house, my mother would sit up in bed and quiz me about Joy. She'd ask where Joy bought her Christmas presents, where Joy had her car serviced, whether the steaks Joy cooked were tasty, like from the butcher shop, or shitty, like from Stop & Shop. I told my mother everything I knew — out of spite mostly, out of the pleasure I took in watching her commit so much energy to so self-destructive a mania. In "starting over," my mother tried to nurture all those things that life with my father had stunted. She wanted to be a voracious reader, a good daughter and sister, a successful interior decorator, a hot date. Still, even as my mother tried to broaden her inner world, her outer world was growing appreciably smaller. Wherever Joy went, my mother couldn't follow. I used to imagine Joy roaming around our house. I'd picture her bouncing up and down on the threadbare floral sofas in the living room, running her hands along the straw wallpaper that lined the hallways, scuffing her feet on the powder-blue shag rug in my mother's bedroom. And I imagined my mother running after her, trying to find a room she hadn't been in, and failing. My mother collated the Joy sightings with her usual brave, don't-pity-me air. But I wondered — as she must have wondered — how she would carry on her new life if she allowed Joy to whittle the world down restaurant by restaurant, room by room.

A couple of days after Christmas, my mother, my sister, and I went to Providence to see my grandmother Almerinda. The ride took an hour and for most of it my sister smoked in the back seat and my mother ate peppermint patties. At one point, my mother thrust the bag at me and said, "Jeff, get these things away from me, will you?"

I put the candies into the glove compartment, and we drove a little farther.

"Okay, just give me *one*," my mother said, and I did. "Now put them back in the glove compartment," she said. "If I ask again, pretend you didn't hear me."

Fifteen minutes later, my mother asked for two more mints; ten minutes after that, she asked for three. Each time, Susan said, "Don't do it, Jeff," but I did it anyway, and then put the bag back into the glove compartment. After that, there was a long stretch of silence, during which my mother seemed poised to ask again, but didn't. Then, just outside Pawtucket, she pulled over to the side of 95, and instructed me to lock the peppermint patties in the trunk.

As we approached my grandmother's dented screen door, my mother took my arm and said, "Jeffrey, do me a favor — do like your sister does and kiss Grandma. Poor thing, she can barely walk." I nodded and went inside. My grandmother was watching wrestling at the kitchen table. Her longtime live-in boyfriend, Ben, whom she met many years after Ercole died of pneumonia, was knocking about in the other room. As a child, I had asked my mother why Grandma and Ben weren't married. She told me they weren't married because of Social Security. I had no idea what she meant — it seemed to me that if they wanted security they *should* get married — but my mother made it clear that I wasn't to bring it up again. For some reason, Ben was not popular with my mother or my Uncle Ricco or even with saintly Uncle Peter. Whenever I asked one of them why, they'd say, "Oh, hey, don't get me started on Ben" or "The kid wants to know about Ben. *You* tell him, Stella."

I liked Ben primarily because nobody else did. I also liked him because he let my grandmother boss him around — based on what little I knew about her life with Ercole, she seemed to have earned that right. When Ben came into the kitchen now, he was wearing blue mechanic-style pants and a sleeveless undershirt. I shook his hand, and approached my grandmother. She was an enormous woman, with a tiny, kindly face. She smelled pleasantly of baby powder; she wore rings on five fingers. She looked like my mother.

I brushed her cheek with my cheek. "Hello, Grandma."

"Jeffrey Matthew," she said, blushing and squeezing the rubber grips on her walker. "I didn't think you'd come."

"Hi, Mama. You look real good," my mother said, running her hand through her mother's fine, newly permed hair.

Susan approached Grandma, threw her arms around her and kissed her exuberantly on both cheeks. "Hey,

sexy!" she said. "Who curled your hair? It looks wicked
nice."

"Oh, some gal down the shop."

"I could have done that, Grandma. I could have done
that for *nothin'*. "

"Next time, Susan Karen. I promise."

"Does your hair stink now?"

"Oh, it really does, yeah," Grandma said.

Susan leaned forward to smell Grandma's scalp. "Not
too bad," she said. "You better watch out, Ben. Grandma's
looking real sexy."

"Ack," Ben said.

We sat down and there were a few moments of silence.
Susan looked at the television. "Grandma, you're into
wrestlin'?"

"Once in a while. You know."

"*Once* in a while!" Ben protested, taking a chair near my
grandmother and patting her head with his plump hand.
"Every Sunday — I don't care if the *Pope* gets shot — she
sits in that chair and watches wrestling."

"Ah, you!" Grandma said, swatting his hand.

"Is that Hulk Hogan?" my sister asked.

"Hulk Hogan *nothing!*" my grandmother said.

There was another silence. We looked around the room:
ladder-back chairs with vinyl cushions, brightly colored
plastic placemats, nothing you couldn't clean with a
sponge. On the wall behind the television was a crucifix
covered with a plastic bag and a wall hanging called "In
the Doghouse." Attached to it were five or six small
wooden dogs, each brightly painted and affixed with a
name tag — Peter, Ricco, Susan, etc. My mother first explained this to my sister and me by saying, "It's a shit list.

You're mad at somebody? You take their dog, you put it in the doghouse."

Susan looked at the wall. "Ben, you're always in the doghouse," she said.

"I know it. Don't think I don't."

"I mean, we've been coming here, like, ten years. How come you're always in the doghouse?"

"Ack. Who knows? Maybe because I walk in front of the TV. Ask your grandmother."

"Grandma, how come Ben's always in the doghouse?"

"Susan Karen, don't get me started."

There was a long pause, during which all of our minds whirred in search of something to talk about. My grandmother asked my mother how St. Anthony's was.

"It's okay, I guess."

"You guess? What does that mean, you *guess?*"

"Well, Mama, to tell you the God's honest truth . . ."

"Oh Jesus God. What? You don't go to church no more? You're not a Roman Catholic?"

"Well, Mama, I've been shopping around."

"Shopping around? What does that mean, shopping around?"

"I met an Episcopalian minister. And there's some Buddhists in Hingham."

"There's some Buddhists in Hingham? So don't go to Hingham."

"I talked to a couple of Unitarians."

"This I don't believe. Now you're talking to Unitarians? Those people believe in *nothing*, Susan. Couldn't have been a long conversation." Grandma paused. "Why aren't you going to St. Anthony's no more?"

"Ma, Glen goes to St. Anthony's."

Susan corrected her: "*Joy* goes to St. Anthony's, Grandma."

"Oh Jesus God," Grandma said to my mother. "Your ex-husband — I never liked his hair. You got to meet somebody new."

"I'm trying, Mama. I got gas station guys asking me out. I don't really want to talk about it."

"Pretty Italian girl like you — "

"I don't want to talk about it, Mama."

"All I'm saying — "

"Leave her alone, Almerinda," Ben said.

Grandma looked at Ben. "Ah, *you!*" she said.

More silence. I never knew what to say to my relatives. At times like this, my mother didn't seem to either. After Auntie Anna died in the car accident in 1975, we saw them so seldom that we lost all semblance of a common ground. Our visits were like a scene in one of those Chinese movies where an immigrant generation returns to their homeland and shocks their grandparents with Walkmen and Reeboks. What was strange was that my family had never migrated. We lived an hour away. Whatever gulf there was between my mother and her family was caused not by distance but by neglect. My mother blamed herself, but she blamed my father more. Why had she married a man who wasn't Italian? A man who, for years, wouldn't even *talk* to his own father? A man who sat by and watched his family's silver get sold at auction?

My mother, shrugging off the awkwardness of the moment, slid her car keys across the table at me. I looked up. She smiled.

"Don't do it, Jeff," Susan said.

"Don't do what?"

"Jeff, honey?" my mother said. "I think you left something in the trunk."

Two hours later, my mother had turned the table into a field of York peppermint patty wrappers — some of them crushed into balls, some flattened smooth, some twisted into shiny, little abstract sculptures — and I was incalculably bored and antsy. The knowledge that I couldn't just jump in my Pinto and drive over to Alan's or Joe's always brought on feelings of powerlessness and dread. As a child, I would stand at the Stop & Shop checkout while my mother ran off to grab some just-remembered item. I'd watch as the cashier rang up the Parmesan cheese, the Pixie Stix, the yogurt, the Pop Rocks, the angel hair pasta, the wheat bread, and the Koogle peanut butter. As the pile in our cart shrank, I'd grow cold and clammy with the knowledge that the cashier would shortly be asking me to produce either my mother or my mother's pocketbook and that, failing both, I'd be placed under arrest. Other times, my mother would double-park outside a shop and position me in the driver's seat as a decoy. Again, that feeling of powerlessness would creep over me. Someone that my mother had parked in would return and start honking. I'd pretend I didn't hear him, and he'd bolt out of his car, livid. I'd watch in the rearview mirror as he stalked up to my window. When he saw that I was eleven years old, his face would fall and he'd go off in search of a tow truck or a meter maid or somebody qualified to arrest me.

My mother always reappeared seconds before the cashier rang up the last item or the irate driver returned with a

SWAT team. Now, though, she was delighted to see me trapped. The sooner I wanted to leave, the longer she wanted to stay. At one point during this interminable afternoon — while Grandma and Ben were carrying on one argument and my mother and Susan were conducting another — I took the phone into the bathroom and called Joe. The phone had been adjusted with my grandmother's hearing in mind so that Joe's "'lo?" came over the line in a distorted burst. I lowered the volume.

"Witless?" I said.

"I'm sorry, Mr. Whittle is in the sauna with Cheryl Tiegs. This is his male secretary, may I help you?"

"I'm at my grandmother's house, big guy."

"Dude, you're bumming."

"No shit."

Just then, Joe's mother picked up a phone in the living room and said, "Hello?"

"I got it," Joe said.

"Who is it?"

"I *got* it."

"I'm just asking who it is, Joseph."

"Hang up! Hang up! Hang up!"

Joe's mother hung up, and Joe said, "*Jesus.*" As we talked, I noticed that there was a seat built into my grandmother's shower. I got in and sat down. I could still hear voices yelling in the next room, so I slid the glass door shut.

"What am I doing here?" I said, my voice echoing in the shower stall.

"You fucked up," Joe said. "You should have taken your own car. I always take the Bug — even if we're going across the street. Because they *tell* you they're going to Mickey-D's, and then it's like, 'Oh, and we just gotta stop at the drugstore and the bank.' Fuck that."

Suddenly, there was a commotion on the line. Joe's mother had picked up the downstairs phone and was dialing. Joe tried to get her attention between each digit, but couldn't. We listened to the dial tumble around seven times, and then Joe shouted, "Hang up or die!"

"Oh, are you still on the phone, Joseph?"

"Oh my God. Yes, I am still on the phone."

"Will you tell me when you're off?"

"You'll know I'm off, Mother, 'cause I'm gonna come downstairs and murder you."

Joe's mother went to hang up, but was flustered and missed the cradle on the first two passes. There were two or three seconds of rattling, and then, mercifully, peace. Joe and I resumed our conversation. Minutes later, however, my own mother came into the bathroom and slid the shower door open. "Jeffrey," she said, "what in the hell are you doing?"

"Tell her to kiss your ass," Joe said, on the other end of the line.

"Kiss my ass."

"Jeffrey!"

"*Awesome!*"

"Is that Joseph Whittle? Hang up this instant. Your Uncle Peter just pulled up."

"Joe, Uncle Peter's here. I have to cruise."

"Dude, Uncle Peter can kiss my ass."

When my mother and I returned to the kitchen, Uncle Peter was standing at the table and brushing peppermint patty wrappers into a green plastic garbage pail. My mother walked over to help him. Uncle Peter hugged her flamboyantly, briefly rocking back and forth on both feet, and kissed her on the cheek. "How ya doing, kiddo?" he said. "How's the job? How's the house?" He paused. "Met anybody?"

That night, my mother called to ask if I'd help her write a personal ad.

"Absolutely not."

"Why not, Jeffrey?"

"I just won't."

"Jeffrey, I can't do it myself. I read these things and it's like, 'DWF seeks . . .' I don't even know what these initials stand for. Half of them — they sound like airports. Listen to this: 'GWM seeks discreet — ' "

"I don't think you want to answer that one, Mom."

"So you'll help me?"

"No."

"Jeffrey!"

"I *will* not write a personal ad for my mother. It's too creepy."

"Oh, I see. It's okay for your father to cart the Slut all over town — to bring her into St. friggin' Anthony's — but I'm supposed to sit at home. That really sucks, mister."

"It's not that I want you to sit at home — "

"Look, Jeff. I've got to do something with myself. I've got to make a change. Just 'cause *you* think I'm an old lady — "

"I don't think you're an old lady, Mom. But I won't write

your personal ad. You've already got gas station attendants asking you out. Now you want to get letters from inmates?"

"Well, Jeff, I'm going to do it. And I can't do it alone. I can't describe myself. All these ladies are so full of bull. 'Gorgeous, fiftyish woman with smart figure . . .' Yeah, sure. I feel like writing 'Fat, slovenly pig . . .' Just to see, you know? Just to see what would happen."

"Well, that's a start. 'FSP seeks same.' "

"Do you think I'm a fat pig, Jeffrey?"

"I'm hanging up now, Mom."

"Don't hang up — you know I'll just call you back. Jeff, write this thing for me. Please. It won't take fifteen minutes."

"I'm hanging up, Mom, and I'm taking my phone off the hook."

During the conversation, I stepped outside myself again and looked on. Why was I acting like a jerk? My mother was trying to lurch ahead, to start over, and, as always, I saw only the hopelessness of it all. During the next few months, she brought up the personal ad regularly. I'd arrive home from school and there would be a recent eight-by-ten of my mother on my desk and a fresh piece of paper in my typewriter that read, "Fiftyish gal seeks . . ." I'd come down to the kitchen at night, and my mother would accost me: Why was I so embarrassed by her? Didn't I think she could get a date? What did she have to do to get my approval — find a steady job, learn how to sail, talk with a British accent, stop eating peppermint patties? Well, forget that happy horseshit, mister.

A week before my mother's birthday, I asked her what

she wanted and she said, "A hundred bucks." I said, "What for?" and she said, "Never mind what for." So one day Joe, Alan, and I drove down to the Pilgrim Cooperative Bank, where I wrote a check to "Cash" and was given in return five crisp, whispering twenties. We then went to Cards & Shards where I bought a birthday card, which I signed without reading. I slipped the bills inside the card and the card inside the envelope. We drove back up Pleasant Street to my house. I gave my mother the card. She read it and started to cry. Did I really mean it? Of course I did. My mother hugged me. She hugged Joe. She hugged Alan. Then we said, "Okay, see you later," and went over to Joe's to play "Spanish Bombs," "Same Old Song and Dance," and "Pearl Necklace." During one of Joe's endless drum solos, it struck me that a hundred dollars was a lot to pay for a personal ad. Then it struck me — and the thought seemed inconceivably sad — that my mother assumed no one would answer her ad and that she'd have to run it week after week.

One night in March, my father and I went to see a movie and he fell asleep after fifteen minutes. I knew because his head had fallen back and his face was turned up toward the ceiling like somebody whose throat had been cut. He began to snore — a thin, far-off rattle that rose and fell regularly like a sine wave. I nudged my father and he shuddered, rubbed his eyes, and squinted at the film for a minute. Somebody was standing at a window in an airport, watching an airplane take off.

"What kind of plane is that, Tiger?" my father whispered.

"A 727," I said.

"That's affirmative," my father murmured. Soon he was asleep again, his body curved forward and his head down between his knees, like somebody prepared for a crash landing.

These days, my father and I spent most of our time talking about college — about how I'd be the first person on either side of the family to graduate, about how he'd flunked out of Cornell, about how I shouldn't think it'd be an easy ride like high school, and about how I'd better steer clear of the liberals. For the last year or so, I had had the idea that if I got into a "good" college, it would somehow erase the past. Suddenly, nobody would care that, while I'd made As in some classes, I was functionally illiterate in the sciences and routinely brought home Cs and Ds in calculus and physics. College, I reasoned, would be my own chance to start over. And, with this in mind, I took on anything that might make the colleges think I was a student leader. I was president of the school band (which was dreadful) and co-editor of its newspaper (which rarely came out because Alan and I were the only ones willing to write for it). I was a member of the National Honor Society; I was on the staff of the yearbook; I ran cross-country. Everything I did, though, was halfhearted. As I've said, my mother and I lived near the high school, and during cross-country practice we'd run by my house. I was always a quarter of a mile behind the next slowest runner, and when the team dipped out of sight down my hill, I'd duck into my house, microwave a Cup-a-Soup, and watch TV until practice was over. I never told my dad any of this. Instead, I'd just listen to him talk about Cornell, or I'd recite, at his request, my impressive-sounding credentials. My father would then nod and say, "Good man, Jeff. Good man."

Around this time — the spring of 1983 — my sister and my mother also set about reestablishing their relationship. Which is to say they sat around bitching about my father and Joy. I'd come across them in our living room, and they'd be laughing and drinking Kahlua. Seeing them together made me nervous, frankly — they were like two superpowers forging a secret alliance. When my mother saw me in the doorway, she'd invite me to sit down.

"Jeff doesn't drink, Ma. Jeff's a lewsa," Susan would say.

"Your brother is not a loser," my mother would announce in mock seriousness. "Jeff, you sure you don't want a Kahlua, sweetie?"

"I'm sure," I'd say, leaving the room.

When they thought I was out of earshot, my mother would lean forward and whisper, *"Loser,"* and the two of them would burst into high, girlish squeals.

By the time the movie was over, my father was snoring loudly and his body was craned halfway into the aisle. I had to wake him up so that people could get by. My father awoke with a start. He shook his head back and forth, as if he'd been punched, and he looked up at the screen and saw that the final credits were rolling. "Did I fall asleep?" he said.

We walked out to the Pinto. I had offered to drive because I was hoping my father would notice what an unsightly, broken-down piece of junk the Pinto was and offer to buy me a new car. He didn't. Instead, we drove home arguing about how loud the stereo should be and talking about colleges. When we pulled up at Forest Avenue, I turned the car off and Joy and Susan could suddenly be heard shouting in the house. My father lowered his head. "Want to come in?" he asked.

"No, I'd better run," I said.

"I don't blame you. Susan's been going through some bad times. Trying to get a job, that kind of thing."

"Dad, Susan goes through *nothing* but bad times."

"She's your flesh and blood, Jeff."

"Oh, please. What's with Joy, anyway?"

"She's upset about the house. You know, it's just taking me so long. We've still got wires hanging out of the walls. Someday, your old man's going to get electrocuted while he's sitting on the john."

My father opened his door. "Anyway, good seeing you, Tiger. I've got to go play referee."

He got out and closed the Pinto's door, which creaked as it shut. For a moment, my father leaned in through the window. "Ford makes a damned good car," he said, and disappeared into his house.

At two A.M. that night, I was woken by some noise in the kitchen. I got out of bed and went into the hall where, disoriented by sleep, I crashed into the humidifier and then fell against the opposite wall, the photographs on which were still clattering when I went down the steps toward the kitchen. Soon, I smelled something sweet — incense, maybe — and I could hear the sounds in the kitchen more clearly. There was giggling, there was the sound of newspapers rustling, there was the faint clicking of scissors.

I stopped outside the door. The room seemed impossibly bright. My mother was sitting in one of the ladder-back chairs, which in turn sat on the comics section of a *Boston Sunday Globe*. Her hair was wet and she was wearing a canary-yellow T-shirt that read, "If We Can Send One Man to the Moon, Why Can't We Send Them All?" Susan was barefoot and cutting my mother's hair. She paused momentarily to take a hit from a joint. The joint was tiny and Susan held it with eyebrow tweezers. After passing it to my mother, she waited a few seconds, then released a funnel of smoke. Susan bent down to scratch the bottom of her foot, which was black with newsprint. She took a long drink from a Flintstones glass that was resting on the table, then offered the glass to my mother. My mother coughed harshly and beat her chest, sending pockets of smoke out of her mouth in all directions. She grabbed for the glass. My sister and my mother giggled, then started rummaging through a Mister Donuts box. Susan picked a jelly doughnut topped with granulated sugar and my mother picked a glazed one with pink frosting and sprinkles.

They ate for a while and then Susan went back to cutting my mother's hair. The last thing I noticed as I turned back toward my room was that on the far side of the kitchen, in a heap, were three of my sister's suitcases, her hair dryer, and her alarm clock, which was still decorated with a row of crude, nail-polish-red roses.

Susan began staying over. Everything went smoothly because it was tacitly understood that the arrangement was temporary. Susan would stay as long as she needed in order to get it together, then one day Dad and Joy would come for her and she'd go. And, for the first time, it seemed as if Susan *was* getting it together. She found a job at a John Delaria salon in Quincy. She greeted customers, shampooed their hair, gave them a towel, and introduced them to their stylist. Susan liked the salon and was working hard so she'd get promoted.

My mother had also gotten a steady job; she was an office manager for a balding, Weeble-shaped ophthalmologist in Kenmore Square. These were good days for both Susan and my mother, and, early in April, I myself got a long-awaited mailboxful of responses from various colleges. (Princeton, for whom I had completed not one but two applications, rejected me.) For twenty minutes, I sat on one of the floral velvet sofas in the living room and pored over the letters. I decided to go to Brown University and when I called my mother at work to tell her, she was thrilled — not only because Brown had been my first choice, but also because it was in Providence, which meant I could finally spend some time with Grandma and Uncles Peter and Ricco. My mother asked if I'd do that for her. I said that I would. I said, "I love you," and hung up. Then I sat back down on the sofa and thought about how I'd wanted to leave Cohasset for so long but how, until now, I'd had nowhere to go.

Of the three of us spending peaceful days at Reservoir Road, my mother was the most transformed. Now that she had a steady income, she began saving money for the interior design business she'd been talking about for years. In my cynicism, I used to find it odd that my mother thought she was capable of decorating other people's houses when ours was such an eyesore. She'd drape huge swatches of rough blue silk over our living room chairs. She'd tack ivory-colored wallpaper over the straw-

mat paper in her bedroom. She'd strewn the blue shag
rug in the hallways with enormous books of carpet sam-
ples. For her first full-scale experiment in decorating, my
mother chose my bathroom. It is a longish, narrow room.
For the life of me, I can't remember what it looked like
before my mother set siege to it. The refinished room —
preserved to this day, like the dining room of a Founding
Father — is covered with a garish, metallic paper featur-
ing brown-and-orange leaves. The paper is not only on
the walls but on the ceiling so that the bathroom looks
something like a Christmas present. On either side of the
bathroom mirror are vertical rows of bright round lights
of the sort one might find in a stripper's dressing room.

My mother was still collecting Joy sightings. As they
accumulated — as the number of stores and restaurants
my mother could safely patronize dwindled — the house
on Reservoir Road became an obsession for her. She spent
her evenings drawing diagrams and taking measure-
ments, deciding which of our plain rooms she'd descend
upon once she'd saved more money. My mother didn't
seem concerned about the world outside the house as long
as she had the world inside it. In truth, she didn't seem
concerned about anything. She was slimmer and happier.
She seemed to have made her "change," whatever it was. I
no longer heard her turning pages at all hours of the
night; I no longer found a trail of peppermint patty wrappers everywhere I went; and, when my mother dialed the
phone in her room, it no longer rang in mine. I assumed
that my mother had had some luck with her personal ad,
and I was happy for her, but I didn't particularly want
to hear about it, so I didn't ask. Instead, I helped out
around the house as much as I could. I Pintoed all over

Cohasset on a dizzying number of errands. I went every-where my mother refused to go: to the Kit & Kaboodle for candles, to the butcher for steak, to Curtis Compact for ketchup and bread.

Soon it was Easter Sunday, and my mother and I had dinner with Susan, Mike, Lonnie, Kip, Sarah the hypno-tist, my friend Bill Davenport, somebody named Ronald whom *nobody* knew, and Mr. and Mrs. Lodge. There were too many of us to sit at the dining room table, so my mother set up a buffet in the kitchen. Susan and the Lodges camped out on a sofa. Ronald, Kip, and Sarah sat in a semicircle of chairs. Bill and I crouched on the blue shag rug. My mother was in fine form all afternoon. She raced around giddily, humming a bouncy tune that she apparently thought of as her theme song. She refilled glasses the second she heard the clicking of ice cubes; she swayed her hips; she whisked away dirty plates. Every five minutes, she pulled someone upstairs to look at the re-decorated bathroom, and the person would return shak-ing his or her head and saying ambiguously, "It's really something, Jeff. Isn't that something?"

"Yes," I'd say. "But *what?*"

Bill was the only exception. He had a few too many of my mother's mimosas — champagne, a touch of Grand Marnier or Triple Sec, and just enough Tropicana to turn the drink orange — and he told her that the bathroom looked like a stripper's dressing room.

"Bill!" Susan said. "You're cruising for a bruising."

To everyone's relief, my mother laughed. "Bill," she said, "I think I'll make you wash the dishes."

*

Early in May, I came home from marching band and found Susan's suitcases in a pile near the door. Minutes later, she came downstairs with her pocketbook. "Hey, Jeff," she said.

"Hey, Sue," I said.

"You look wicked dweeby," she said. I was wearing my band uniform: white polyester pants with blue racing stripes and bell-bottom cuffs; a white "alligator" shirt; a blue blazer with the words "Cohasset Skippers" sewn onto a chest pocket; a blue and white military-style hat; and a pair of shiny black shoes.

"Yeah," I said. I removed my hat. "So, you taking off?"

"Uh-huh. Dad and Joy are coming to get me."

"You bummed?" I said, noticing that when I talked to my sister, I spoke the way she spoke.

"No. Ma and I — Anyway, my job's going pretty good so I'm outta there this summer."

"Cool," I said.

"Yeah," Susan said. "I don't want to fuck Ma up or anything. I think she's doing real good, you know?"

"Must be the personal ad," I said.

"No, she never bought one."

"What?"

"She had a hard time writing the thing so she blew it off. She hasn't had a date in months. Don't tell her I said that. She gets wicked bummed about it."

I looked at Susan a moment. "What did Mom do with the hundred bucks I gave her?"

"You gave her a *hundred* bucks? What did you give me for *my* birthday? A hairbrush or something?"

"No, I — "

"I'm just shitting you, Jeff. You're so clueless."

The news about my mother surprised me, and I felt my stomach drop at the thought of how petty I'd been in refusing to help her. I didn't say anything for a while. Soon, my father's peeling gold Cadillac pulled up. He turned off the engine, but it was still bucking and chortling as he and Joy got out. Closing his door, my father laughed and pointed a finger at the car and said, "*Stay.*"

Susan and I walked out onto the porch. Dad and Joy were wearing their USAir uniforms, and when they saw my band outfit they did a double take.

"Nice slacks, Tiger," my father said.

"Nice hat, Captain."

"You ready, love?" Joy asked Susan. "Can we help?"

Joy made a move for the door, and suddenly my old mental images of her bouncing up and down on my mother's sofa and scuffing her feet on my mother's rug flashed across my mind. These images quickly led to a new one: Joy walking out of my mother's brown-and-orange bathroom and shaking her head.

Susan and I moved to block the door. "We can manage," Susan said.

Alan danced with Kimberly Douglas. He danced with her during one of the "disco nights" held in the C.H.S. cafeteria. Joe and I hadn't wanted to go — there were never any girls we liked and we always ended up sitting in a corner and playing air guitar. Still, it was the last dance of the year and, since Joe never had any money, Alan had offered to pay his way. When we arrived at the cafeteria — Alan and I were wearing sweaters and Joe, whose hair was wet and scrupulously parted, was wearing his jean jacket and a pink dress shirt — all the tables and chairs had been pushed to one side of the room. "China Grove" was seguing into "China Girl," and the darkened room was pulsating with blue and white, the school's colors. There was a revolving mirrored ball and a deejay with a red bandanna tied around his head, who was shouting things like "Party down, people" and "*Let* it loose. *Let* it loose."

Joe and I made a beeline for a corner, sat down, and started playing air guitar. Most people play air guitar half-heartedly — their right hand strumming absentmindedly, their left hand frozen in a Dr. Strangelove clutch. Joe and I bent imaginary strings, pumped imaginary tremolo bars, and held imaginary guitars up to imaginary amps for distortion. If Joe saw that we were both miming the solo, he'd stop and refuse to play until I had switched to bass.

While Joe and I were goofing around, Alan was scanning the room for Kimberly. Before long, he spotted her: she was wearing an oversize white dress shirt and gray slacks, and dancing with J.P. Turner. Every so often, J.P., who was short but bulky and wearing a Members Only windbreaker and painter's pants, would climb a nearby steel pole, shake his fist a couple of times, then climb back down and resume dancing.

"I can't stand to watch this," Alan shouted over the music.

"Cut in," I shouted back.

"If J.P. gives you a hard time, we'll kick his ass," Joe said.

"Yeah, right," Alan said. "He'd waste us."

The deejay played a Tom Petty tune, then something by Joe Jackson, and then something by Elvis Costello. Alan finally got up his nerve. He stood and started walking toward Kimberly. When "Heartache Tonight" came on, he came lurching back.

"*Big* guy," I screamed, crestfallen.

"I refuse to dance to the Eagles," Alan said.

The next thirty minutes were wasted with two couples-only slow songs and a dance contest, during which J.P. Turner induced everyone to flop down on their backs and writhe around as if they were receiving electric shocks. My mind was wandering. I was thinking about my mother and feeling guilty. I was thinking that I'd been treating my life with her as just another of our haywire conversations — something that was beyond my control, something that followed a script long since written.

"Alan," I shouted. "The dance is going to be *over* in ten minutes."

Joe nodded. "And the last song is going to be fuckin' 'Freebird.' "

"She won't dance with me anyway," Alan said.

"Why not?" I said.

"Because I'm a loser," Alan said. "And I hang out with losers."

"Harsh!" I said. "I think you're forgetting Joe's a stud."

"Look at us," Alan said. "We don't drink. We don't smoke."

"We rock and roll!" Joe said.

"No, *you* guys rock and roll," Alan said. "I hit things against my forehead."

"You're a poet," Joe said. "You write for the *Lamplight Literary Magazine*."

"Thanks, Joe," Alan said. "You just made it worse."

"He's right, Witless," I said. "We're losers. We've fallen off the high school food chain."

"This is bullshit," Joe said. "I put on a pink shirt for this? Alan, if you don't dance with her, *I'm* going to. And I swear to God I'll squeeze her butt."

"Freebird" came on. Alan got up and charged toward Kimberly, and Joe and I shouted after him, "Let it loose, Alan! *Let* it loose!" In the pulsing strobes, everybody on the dance floor looked as if they were break-dancing. Joe and I couldn't hear what Alan said to Kimberly — and he refused to tell us later — so we could only watch as he took her arm and guided her around J.P., who was now spinning on his head.

When I came home that night — my ears still ringing from the dance — my mother was asleep in the living room. Her head had fallen to one side and her chest was working slowly and regularly. On the coffee table in front of her was her old Sony tape recorder. I walked in quietly, lifted the recorder off the table, and carried it up to my room.

Once upstairs, I shut my door and put on one of Brian Eno's *Ambient* albums. As the music came over the speakers — droning, watery, oddly weightless — I rewound my mother's tape halfway and pressed Play. The tape was of a woman's hushed voice — a voice I recognized but couldn't place. The voice was saying, "There is only my voice. There are no other sounds. Your neck muscles are relaxing. Your stomach muscles are relaxing. Your eyelids are closed because they're heavy. Your eyelids are heavy. Your breathing is relaxed and deep — not uncomfortably deep — but just relaxed and deep."

Sarah Thompson, I thought. The hypnotist. I pressed Fast Forward. A moment later, Sarah was saying, "You're getting better, Susan. Always getting better — every day, in every way. Whether it's your work or your family or just driving your car. But you know that. You already know that. Getting better. Always better. Remember my voice, Susan. You're breathing deeply now. All your muscles have let go."

Fast Forward. Play. "You know you're getting better, Susan. We don't need to concentrate on that. That's no longer an issue. What we need to concentrate on — listen only to my voice — is the problem we talked about in my office. When you're having that problem, you'll place your hand on your stomach and you'll count to three. One. Two. Three. Slow and quiet. Quiet and slow. And you won't have the problem anymore. The thought will be unappealing to you — not repulsive, not anything like that — just unappealing. Your taste buds will become supersensitive to that taste, and you know the taste I'm talking about. You will not want peppermint patties, Susan. You will not want peppermint patties."

When I went downstairs to replace the tape recorder, my mother had not moved. I sat down and watched her a moment, listening to the wind and the thwack of the bushes as they beat against the back of the house. I thought that she looked pretty. I thought, also, that none of us had been through as much as my mother and none of us had asked for as little. Hours later, the clicking of my typewriter would wake her up, as I sat composing her personal ad. Until then, my mother's breathing would be slow and quiet, quiet and slow. She'd sleep as deeply as my father ever slept.

I V

THIS IS THE SEA

"I DON'T KNOW where you heard that, Tiger. Actually, I do know where you heard it, but I *never* stopped speaking to my father. That clear? When he left my mother for Liz, I felt some antagonism, yes. I felt betrayed, yes. That's affirmative. Why shouldn't I? You remember when I told you I was going to marry Joy? You were apoplectic. Well, OK, you've forgotten, but I *did* tell you. You were fifteen. I walked in your bedroom one night — 2100 maybe — and I said, 'I'm thinking of marrying this girl.' You got very upset. Said, 'Don't do it.' I said, 'Well, son . . .' You said, '*Don't* do it.' It was a survival thing for you — and I don't mean that as a put-down. Nobody else in Cohasset was divorced. Everybody else's family was happy. As far as *you* knew. You didn't know anybody but Todd Burke at that point, and Todd's parents were still together. I don't know if they ever spoke to each other, but they were *together*. Anyway, to make a long story short, you got very upset and then *I* got upset. I'd told your sister a couple of weeks earlier, and she'd been ecstatic about the whole thing. You know Susan, *anything* to cross your mother. But you just sat on your bed and said, 'Don't do it, Dad. Please don't do it.' You didn't say anything else.

"And that's how it was when my father told me about Liz. Come to think of it, I might have taken it even harder. Remember: your mother and I were divorced when I

157

decided to marry Joy. Your mother and I weren't living together and I had butchered our relationship — just *butchered* it — beyond recognition. Whereas, my folks *were* still married, they *were* still living together. On top of which, my mother had just had a mastectomy. In those days, having a mastectomy — first of all, very few people survived it, and it was positively grim. On my mother's right side, where she had lost the breast, there was nothing left but her rib cage. There was no such thing as prosthetics and all this bit. There was only her rib cage. It had saved her life but — and I'm trying to be totally honest with you — it was awful looking.

"So my mother really was a sexual cripple when my father left her. Follow? She couldn't very well go out and horse around. She couldn't — She couldn't *offer* herself to someone else. And she took my father's leaving very, very hard. In fact — See, my mother didn't have the greatest disposition in the world to begin with. She was a stubborn woman. She was a fighter. So when my father said he was leaving, she took a kitchen knife to him and said, 'No, you *ain't.*' Well, he left anyway. I wasn't going to stop speaking to my father because of it, but I certainly wasn't going to eat, drink, and get shitty with him and Liz. I made a visit — a duty call — every six months. Your mother came with me once or twice. I'd make small talk, and then I'd get up and leave. No big deal.

"I was also upset at Gramps — at my grandfather — but there again I did not cut off communication. Gramps disowned my father for marrying Liz, which was asinine. And then he had the nerve to tell my mother to get out of town. She was a divorcée and he thought she'd drag the family down. He thought he was an important person. He wasn't. He was a nobody. But he told my mother that I was dirty — I was young and I'd been playing in the street — and he told her to go live on Martha's Vineyard. He even offered to pay her way. Well, my mother cursed him out, of course. In those days, Martha's Vineyard was the boonies, and she damn well knew it.

"But I still made duty calls to Gramps. Every six months. You know why? Because I wanted his house. Pure and simple. I wanted to get his house so I could give it to my father. My father adored the place. So I made my duty calls. But pretty soon there was so much going on with your mother and me that I started putting off the visits. I lost the thread. I didn't see Gramps for a while and he died.

"One day, we drove up by his place and — you may even remember this — and they were auctioning off his things. Well, I got out of the car. You remember the red Cougar? Beautiful piece of work, that car. I got out of the Cougar. I went up to the cashier and I said, 'I'm Glen Giles. That name mean anything to you?' The woman said, 'Yes,' because she knew *exactly* who I was. And I said, 'Well, what's the story?' She told me that Gramps had left everything to Abbey Hayes and Abbey Hayes had — It's a long, convoluted story. The long and short of it was that Lincoln Hayes had died intestate. There was nothing I could do. Your mother wanted to stay and buy various things — Dresden, I think. But I wasn't about to sink a dime into the place. I wasn't going to buy back things that were ours in the first place. So I basically told your mother, '*Get* in the car, woman,' and she did. In those days, we had some friction but — I realize that this is a hell of a way to put it — but in those days your mother obeyed me. When I said 'Black,' *she* said 'Black.' When I said, 'Jump,' she said 'How high?'

"Back then — 'seventy, 'seventy-one — we had some happy times. I don't know if your mother would admit to that or not. What started us downhill, I think, were the fights over you and Susan. Little things. I wanted you kids to say, 'Yes, sir.' No big deal. It's just better than 'Yes.' I wanted 'Yes, *something*.' Yes, Daddy. Yes, Mommy. Not just 'Yes.' Well, as far as your mother was concerned, it flat wasn't going to be that way.

"So that's how things were. What else? Susan used to touch her food to see if it was warm. I told her not to do it. Repeatedly. But your mother would say, 'Susan, you can touch your food if you want to.' Now, Jesus Christ. Excuse my language. I tried to keep my mouth shut. I honest to God tried. Then one night, I lost my cool and we had a pretty good scene in front of some guests. We sat down to have roast beef. The *second* Susan got her plate, she started playing with her food. I didn't say a word. Our guests were very close friends of Susan's. Bob and Liz Santisi. They'd driven five hundred miles to see us, and I was trying to be civil.

"A couple minutes later, I looked over at your sister and she had picked her roast beef up with both hands. I just looked away. Give me some credit. A couple of minutes *later*, Susan was pressing the roast beef against her face — like she had a black eye or something. So I said — under my breath because I wasn't trying to make a scene — I said, 'Shape up. That clear?' Of course, your mother said, very loudly, 'Susan, you can touch your food if you want to.' So I lost my cool. I grabbed Susan's roast beef and I pressed it against *my* face. It sounds funny now. It was not funny. It was a ridiculous thing for me to do. And you — you hated your father, you were terrified of me, but that's a whole other thing — you started to cry. So you were crying, and Susan — well, needless to say, Susan wouldn't eat the roast beef after I'd touched it. That was fine by your mother — anything, so long as I was the villain. Your mother said, 'Your father's an animal, Susan. I'll go get you another piece.' Well, now I *really* lost it. I pitched a fork across the room and nearly got Liz Santisi with it. Again, it sounds funny. It was not funny.

"So where raising you children was concerned, your mother — God bless her, but she's stubborn as hell — your mother bucked me every step of the way. And then there was the simple fact that you kids were more important than I was. You got attention when *I* wanted attention. And I *could not* tolerate that. Pure and simple. I wrecked your bedroom in New Hartford one time. Remember that? The room needed to be redone. Usually, I'd only wreck things that needed to be fixed anyway. So your mother and I — Well, you're a grown-up, Jeff, I'll tell you. Your mother and I were making love. In the middle of our making love, you started crying. I don't remember why. So your mother gets up and rushes down the hall to dote on you. I didn't think it would kill you to cry for five minutes, but your mother flat wouldn't have it. So she gets up and rushes down the hall, and I go after her and end up punching your bedroom walls in. I was jealous of you kids. It was pure pettiness. It's embarrassing to admit that, but I'm trying to be honest with you and at that point in my life that's where I was at.

"So every so often I'd lose my cool. And, as time went on, your mother would lose her cool, too. She'd slam a drawer or she'd break something. She'd get mad and I'd get twice as mad. When you're angry enough, you'll do anything. You don't care what it's going to cost you. OK, not *you*, Tiger, but in general. I had always been like that. Somebody would cut me off on the highway and I'd pull the son of a bitch over. He could be nine feet tall — some guy who could kick the daylights out of me — but I'd chew him out sure as you're a foot high. I had *always* been a fighter. And once your mother became one — well, that's when we really went at it.

"Still, I think we could have survived the fights. Seriously. We had our happy times. The real disaster was the stewardesses. I started nailing stewardesses — that's where I was at — and it wrecked us. It just *wrecked* us. When your mother first figured it out, she took you kids and she drove home to Warwick. I'm sure it was the last thing in the world she wanted to do because, as you may or may not know, she had an abusive father, a father who was a heavy, heavy drinker.

"But your mother went home. What else could she do? So one night your mother's sitting up with her folks — Ercole and Almerinda. You kids are in bed, I guess. So they're sitting there and Ercole's boozing — I drank for years, but frankly this guy scared the *shit* out of me. Excuse my language. Ercole is drinking and out of nowhere he says to your mother, 'Glen only married you so he could fuck you.' Now, that's a hell of a thing to say to your own kid. Your mother's mouth is just hanging open. How do you respond to that? So Almerinda — here's a woman who put up with a *lot* of bullshit in her life, a woman who put up with more bullshit than even my mother put up with. Almerinda heaves a drink in his face. When you're mad enough, you'll do anything. It was a natural reaction. I'd get a few drinks in my face over the years."

*

This Is the Sea

Almerinda died in Providence in the winter of 1987. In my four years at Brown — four years spent on a hill not five miles distant from my grandmother's house — I had seen her perhaps three times. My mother called me frequently while I was at school. She would tell me about her interior design business; about Susan, who was now cutting hair at John Delaria's; about my father, who had moved to Maryland with Joy, but who she claimed still called her up at night to say that he missed her and that he knew they'd be together some day.

"You know your father," my mother would say, sighing. "A real bullshit artist."

My mother's calls invariably ended with a plea for me to visit my grandmother. She'd ask for my pity: "Look, Jeffrey, she can barely walk, poor thing. She's got nobody but that asshole Ben." She'd appeal to my sense of duty: "She's your flesh and blood, Jeffrey." She'd attack my complacency: "She doesn't live but five minutes away. I'll pay for the gas." She'd yell: "You goddamned s.o.b. That woman is not going to live out the year, and I can't believe you're such a selfish shit that you can't spend half an hour watching wrestling."

But I did not go. Where my relatives were concerned, I had always been the odd man out, the reader, the wallflower. For seventeen years, I had sat stone still at family functions. I had worn my Walkman at dinner tables, on porches, and in game rooms. I had rebuffed the kindness of uncles and cousins who wanted me to play Ping-Pong, to check out maps of the solar system, to take Tinkerbell for a walk. Every moment of every visit I had behaved like a stuck-up brat and hated myself for it. I felt perpetually tense — my stomachaches were a running joke among relatives — and when the time finally came to leave I'd be sitting in the cold Toyota while Mom and Susan were still looking for their coats. Now, I felt safely distant from all those dinners and all that anxiety. When my mother called and entreated me to visit Grandma, I'd hem and haw and make excuses. The long and short of it was that I wasn't going to go.

My years at Brown were, almost without exception, good ones. During the spring of '87, which was my last semester, I inexplicably hit the skids and had a protracted bout with insomnia. I would go to bed at midnight. Some nights, I would lie wide awake until six or seven, at which time I'd sleep until eleven. At eleven, I'd get up and shower and dress for my first class, which, mercifully, was not until noon. (Brown, whose elastic, New-Agey curriculum is based on the supposition that the students will challenge themselves, can make for an admittedly easy four years. During orientation week, a dean had warned my freshman class, "Now, a lazy student can breeze through Brown without learning a single thing and without doing any work" and many of us had slumped back in our seats and whispered, "Thank *God*.")

Some nights — instead of lying awake until seven — I would simply drop in and out of sleep at five- and ten-minute intervals, so that I was never quite rested but went through the days on a twitching, hysterical high. When I couldn't sleep, I'd have the same thoughts that all insomniacs must have. I'd think, Well, I'll just hop out of bed and finish off that Semiotics paper! I'll write a poem! I'll call France! I'll do push-ups!

These thoughts would persist for only a moment or two. When I had insomnia, I could not do anything but try —

furiously, vainly — to sleep. I was in a grudge match with Sleep itself. Most nights I spent what seemed like hours trying to understand Sleep so that I might outsmart it. I imagined Sleep as a pond upon which I was a skipping stone. I imagined Sleep as a parking lot in which I could not find a parking place. Some nights — distraught at how slowly the small hours crawled by — my thoughts turned to Time. I imagined Time as a series of doors, and I'd see myself struggling to pull open a door, struggling to gain entrance into the next second. At four in the morning, when I had not had a good night's sleep for weeks, these ruminations seemed brilliant — the insights of a suffering soul. In the daylight, one revealed itself to be more inane than the next.

After a month of sleeplessness, I paid a visit to Brown's Health Services. My fellow students had recently requested that Health Services stockpile "suicide pills" in the event of a nuclear war. And, while the university's doctors did not oblige, I thought that they might be willing to grant a more modest request for sleeping pills. I had a short interview with an unsympathetic, severe-looking nurse who I suspected was a Christian Scientist. She clearly had no intention of giving me anything — even after I had stressed the persistence of my insomnia and discoursed lengthily and, to my mind, quite thoughtfully, on the subjects of Sleep and Time. The severe-looking nurse gave me some suggestions on how to cure my insomnia — one of which was drinking a glass of warm milk before turning in — and then suddenly metamorphosed into a therapist. I grew indignant, and our conversation degenerated.

"How are things at home?" she said.

"Things at home are fine," I said. "It's here that I'm having the problem."

For another week, I tried to sleep. I lived in an ugly, cement-walled barracks of a dormitory called Young Orchard and my room was above a room that belonged to someone named Dave. Dave was a Barry Manilow devotee and every so often he'd play "Mandy" or "Weekend in New England" late into the night. I quickly grew to hate Dave — no doubt this had partly to do with the embarrassment I felt when recalling my own long-dead affection for Mr. Manilow — and to blame him for my insomnia. Now, instead of fixating upon Sleep, I would fixate upon Dave's Slow and Painful Death. In the weeks following my interview with the nurse, I murdered Dave in a hundred ingenious ways.

Eventually, I went to a Store 24 on Thayer Street and bought some Sominex. At first, I was terrified of the pills, but they did put me to sleep — so easily, in fact, that I became terrified of them all over again. Some nights, I would resist the temptation of a pill and instead lie awake all night. Some nights, I would drink a shot of vodka instead. Some nights, certain that I was descending into a murky, Marilyn Monroeish never-never land, I'd knock on my sardonic roommate Evan's door and wake him up in the vain hope that he'd keep me company for an hour or so. After a few minutes, Evan would pull open his door and squint at me. He'd be shirtless, wearing only impossibly tight Ocean Pacific shorts, a gold necklace, and a Dolphins cap beneath which sprouted his bright and wiry red hair. Evan would not be happy to see me. Often, before I could get so much as a sentence out, he would have looked me up and down, surmised that the building was not aflame, and slammed his door, saying only, "Tomorrow you die."

Later, I'd knock on the door of my more charitable roommate, Brian. When Brian opened the door, I'd thrust my foot inside his room and insist that he stay up with me until I fell asleep. Brian would be wearing jockey shorts and his shoulders would be draped with an immense quilt — he'd emerge from his darkened room as if from a sweat lodge, his eyes pink and thin, his hair standing in stiff, wild stalks.

"Evan blow you off?" he'd say sleepily.

"Of course," I'd say.

"All right," Brian would say, nodding his head. "Let's go listen to some tunes."

Brian and I would go to the living room and put in a compact disc. The ritual was always soothing. I had grown up listening to records, and they had long been a source of anxiety. To begin with, there was the problem of the static-charged cellophane. When I had torn it off the record jacket, it clung obstinately to the back of my right hand. Then, once I'd brushed it away, it leapt magnetically to the back of my left hand. Further attempts at displacing the cellophane succeeded only in sending it on a slow crawl down my pant leg. In the end, I gave up and stalked toward the turntable with the plucky remnants of the wrapper clinging to my sock.

Once the record had begun, I held my breath, wincing at each crackle and skip. Over time, the cracks and pops would become a part of the music itself. Even hearing Peter Gabriel's "Games Without Frontiers" on the radio, I subconsciously awaited an infinitesimal click between "Hans plays with Lotte" and "Lotte plays with Jane." Hearing Bruce Springsteen's "Thunder Road," I awaited a skip that would send "Roy Orbison singing for the lonely" careening into "want you only."

Even when compact discs arrived, it took dozens of listenings to erase the memory of those imperfect recordings. Soon, though, every clear, perfect note from a disc sounded like a miracle. On nights when my insomnia was particularly severe, Brian and I would stay up listening to R.E.M. in a stupefied awe. We'd lie on the floor, stare at the flaking cork ceiling, and try to figure out the words to "Fall on Me" or "Sitting Still." In the morning, Evan would lumber into the living room, where Brian and I were still strange, sleeping shapes on the floor. Evan would be wearing a fresh pair of impossibly tight OP shorts and a different Dolphins cap. Coming upon us, he would grin one of his Jack Nicholson grins and wake us up with the words, "And now, Jeffy, you die."

The afternoon I graduated from Brown, I drove to Boston on I-95, ceremoniously dumping my last handful of Sominex out the car window. I did not know what had caused my insomnia but I knew intuitively that it was gone. I watched the sleeping capsules scatter across the highway and I thought of the future, of New York City, of a time when I would turn in early and sleep late, when I would take naps — long, beautiful, utterly pointless naps. I arrived in Cohasset at eleven o'clock that night, and, upon slipping into my faithful bunk bed, lay awake until six, rigid and sleepless.

Three weeks later, two friends and I were residing at 508 Third Street in Hoboken, New Jersey. We were working in New York City — I had gotten a job in the typing pool of a certain high-minded magazine about which too much has already been written — and living in what everyone who saw it described as the Tackiest Apartment on

Earth. The apartment was a split-level. There was a small kitchen downstairs; upstairs were three bedrooms, a living room, and a bathroom, all of which were decorated with a green, deep-pile shag rug, track lighting, and immense wall-to-wall mirrors. The apartment was — there was no mistaking it — a seventies love den. In the late eighties, though, it looked like an empty Nautilus room or an abandoned hair salon. Everywhere one looked, one saw a mirror in which there was a chorus line of one's reflections — the first image was life-size, the others grew smaller and smaller as the line drifted out toward infinity.

In our defense, I can only say that we chose the apartment because it was cheap and because we had spent two long afternoons looking at places that reeked from the exhaust of cars or nearby restaurants, places where the floors were covered with curling, yellowed linoleum, places where one had to walk through someone else's bedroom to get to the bathroom, places where Barry Manilow could be heard coming through a neighboring apartment's walls. We suspected that 508 Third Street had once been the set of a soft-core porn movie — I remember tapping a wall-length bedroom mirror and asking the real estate agent, "Is this two-way?" — but we thought we could live with it.

And we did. More than just suffer the garishness of the place, in fact, we enhanced it. My roommates at the time were Bob Olson and Bill Davenport. Bob, a quiet, square-jawed Brown alum who was inordinately fond of tennis, worked as an actuary. Bill, the friend from Cohasset who told my mother that our bathroom looked like a stripper's dressing room, had just graduated from Dartmouth and started work as a paralegal. Bill had been a philosophy student, but he preferred to be thought of as an outrageous, hard-drinking exhibitionist. He often chased mild-mannered Bob around the apartment in his jockstrap or came home from work at two in the morning, put on a Motorhead disc, and did a demented rain dance around our living room.

Together, Bob, Bill, and I made the apartment even more dreadful with a series of carefully considered purchases. The most sublime of these was a ceramic, cheetah-shaped lamp that Bob brought home early in July. Bob set the cheetah on the living room table. Bill and I circled around it, noting its remarkably lifelike fangs. We told Bob that it was the ugliest thing we had ever seen and that we loved it.

So the early days at 508 Third Street went by like this: Bob leafed through tennis monthlies. Bill chewed tobacco and read Schopenhauer in his fraternity boxer shorts. And, as I spent my days addressing envelopes and filing correspondence, I spent my nights trying to write. I had no earthly idea what I wanted to write about but every night I'd sit at my Macintosh for a couple of hours, creating files called "Part One, Chapter One" and checking out different typefaces. Eventually, I'd get rolling, only to hit a snag. I'd stare at a word for so long that all the blood would run out of it. I'd shunt it aside and type another. Soon, it too would seem curiously empty and unfamiliar . . . and so on until I could not come up with a single word whose definition I was entirely sure of. Fatigued, I would click off the computer, hear its last chiming ping, and retreat to the living room where Bill and Bob were sitting by the light of the cheetah and talking about the fact that we lived in the Tackiest Apartment on Earth.

This Is the Sea

In December, not many months into our settling-in days in Hoboken, my mother called and left this message on our answering machine: "Jeff, honey, it's Mom. Call me." I could tell by the thinness of her voice that she had been crying and, not wanting to deal with her latest crisis, I didn't return the call. Later that night, my mother called again. She told me that Grandma had died and my first reaction, although I'm ashamed to admit it, was to steel myself for what I was certain would be a diatribe about how I was an s.o.b. who wouldn't visit his own flesh and blood. But there was no diatribe. My mother sounded tired; she sounded small. She asked if I could take the train up the following day. It was clear from her tone that she expected me to beg off, to concoct some elaborate excuse. I told my mother I'd take the earliest train. I told her that I loved her and that Grandma had loved her, and I hung up.

That night, I slept and woke, slept and woke. In the morning, I walked down to the cold kitchen, the entrance to which Bill had hung with beads. I made myself toast and cereal but felt too jittery to eat and ended up throwing everything away. A few hours later, I was aboard an Amtrak bound for Providence. I tried to sleep but the shaking of the train kept waking me. I tried to read but my eyes flitted all over the page, refusing to follow the slow march of words. Giving up, I stared out the window and watched the houses of Connecticut go falling by.

As my mother, my sister, and I walked across the parking lot of the funeral home, my mother took my arm and whispered, "Jeffrey, do me a favor? Be nice to your Uncle Peter. That man has *always* been there for me."

171

A moment later, we had reached the entrance and a nondescript, fiftyish attendant in a dark suit pushed open the glass door, saying, "Signatelli?"

"Ceci," my mother corrected him.

The man smiled briefly. "End of the hall on the right," he said. "Leave your coats here."

We walked down the long, colorless hall, passing several parlors, some of which were closed off with plastic, accordion-style sliding doors. Other rooms were open. Outside each, a guest book stood atop a podium. Inside, one could hear the hum and whisper of voices conspiring in a steady but indistinct murmur. We passed quickly. I saw the shine of shellacked caskets and the awkward head-bobbing of receiving lines. When we came to the end of the hall, we found two guest books. One of them, behind which half a dozen slump-shouldered people were waiting, bore the name Signatelli. The other bore the name Ceci. Susan signed the latter book and entered the parlor. My mother followed.

As I approached the book, my eyes scanned down the page without finding a single name that I recognized. I noticed that many names — presumably those of the elderly — were written in a jagged script that resembled a seismograph reading. I noticed how similar my mother's and my sister's signatures were, each attacking the S in Susan with a fierce, downward-slanted stroke. Taking up the pen, I signed "Jeffrey Matthew Giles" in the careful, deliberately legible script I use for bank accounts and other official documents, which bears no relation to my actual signature. I set the pen on the podium, and went in.

Once inside, I felt everyone's eyes on me. I had worn a dark purple, double-breasted sport coat and a polka-dotted tie. I realized instantly that the outfit was a stupid choice, and I cringed at my own image the way one sometimes does when looking in a mirror in a harshly lit dressing room. I put my head down and walked to the casket. Kneeling on the cushioned riser, I felt sleeplessness catch up to me and I put my head in my hands. When I looked up, I saw that the casket was half open and my first thought was that my grandmother looked like a volunteer in a magic act. Looking closer, I saw that her white hair had been curled in tight ringlets, that her pale cheeks had been faintly touched up with rouge, and I was struck with some force by the fact that in death, as in life, she looked so tangibly, so essentially, like my mother.

Before long, Uncle Peter swooped down and led me briskly away from the casket. "How ya doing, kiddo?" he whispered. "How's the job? How's Hoboken? New sport coat?"

I answered Uncle Peter's questions one at a time, and then he leaned close to tell me, "Our mother was a big lady. To be honest, we couldn't find a casket she'd fit in. She was just too big. Finally, I said, 'Geez, isn't there anything you can do?' So they built this contraption. It's gigantic. Frankly, I'm a little worried it won't fit in the hole."

As he led me through the receiving line, Uncle Peter continued to whisper, his voice a distant, wordless buzz in my ear. Once through the line, I hugged my mother for a long time, shaking off the glimmer of her I had seen in Grandma, and I sat down next to my sister. Susan had been crying. I envied her ability to grieve openly just as, years before, I had envied her ability to shake with rage, to knock over kitchen chairs, to shoot through the house shouting. Susan put her hand on my shoulder.

"Jeff, go talk to Ben, would you?" she said. "I feel bad for him. He's wicked lonely and he knows everybody hates him."

We looked across the parlor. Ben was standing at the casket, absentmindedly adjusting Grandma's hair.

"Oh, God," Susan said, sniffling. "He's playing with her wig. Jeff, go talk to him."

"Let's leave him alone a while, OK?"

"Look, don't be a jerk. He's gonna be alone for the rest of his life."

I went to talk to Ben. I asked after his sisters — he has three, although I don't think anyone in the family has ever met them. Ben told me that one of his sisters, Emily, had come in earlier, but that she was worried about the ice on the roads and had left after paying her respects. Ben and I were quiet for a moment.

"Last week, she did nothing but yell," he said. " 'Ben, get me my shoes! Get me my shoes so I can get out of this place! These doctors want my money! Don't they know I got no money?' She wanted me to write a letter to the hospital. A letter of — whaddaya call? — complaint. Ack. I said, 'I don't have any paper, Almerinda.' She said, 'Jesus God, I'll write on *toilet* paper. Get me some toilet paper, Ben!' "

I didn't know what to say to this. I was quiet until Ben started up again.

"The day she died, she was watching a wrestling match," he said. "I got bored and went out to talk to one of the nurses. Two, three minutes maybe. I came back in the room and your grandmother said, 'Ben, damn you, you're so interested in the nurses! Well, don't worry — I'm dying as fast as I can!' I went to sit on her bed, but she just went crazy and kept trying to push me off. She died a couple hours later, and I was still in the doghouse."

Again, I couldn't think of what to say. I felt once more like the child who flees from the scene of his parents' arguments, paralyzed in the face of the whirring, delicate machine that is his family. My eyes flitted nervously around the funeral parlor. Then, as Ben reached into the casket to stroke Grandma's hair, I excused myself and went to sit alone at the back of the parlor. When I looked up at my grandmother's coffin, I saw not one Almerinda but many: the Almerinda who had once touched my father's crew cut with the tips of her fingers, the Almerinda whose husband woke her up to beat her, the Almerinda who shunted Ben around mercilessly.

I started to cry. I cried because I felt ridiculous in my polka-dot tie. Because, across the hall, a long, serpentine line of mourners stood waiting to pay their respects to Mr. Signatelli and here, in my grandmother's parlor, not a soul was kneeling and people were already bored and talking about food. Because I wanted so badly to sleep. Because I felt myself being pulled back into something. Because Grandma, whom I had never really known, was gone from the world and because she had looked so much like my mother.

By now, half the receiving line was staring at me, openly astonished. I fought an impulse to walk out of the room. Instead, I put my face in my hands and convulsed. Soon, I felt the line of chairs sink on either side of me. Without looking up, I knew that my sister was at my left and that my mother — warm and close — was at my right.

"The stewardesses wrecked us. There's not a doubt in my mind. If I had just — Even if I had worked for another airline. At other airlines, they split the crews up for this very reason. The stewardesses R.O.N. at different hotels — in different *towns*, in some cases — so the temptation isn't there. Because if you get a thirty-day trip you've got fourteen nights out with the same crew. You become family. It all just falls together. And it's awful easy to say, 'Let's fly this trip next month.' Well, then you're dead. You get attacked by some nineteen-year-old named Cindy and your wife's five months pregnant and — and you're dead.

"The excuse used to be: I cheat on my wife because she screams at me. The truth is that she screams at you *because* you cheat on her. Still, it's a great excuse and we all used it. Some guys would suffer tremendous amounts of remorse. Some guys wouldn't give a damn. They'd say, 'That's the breaks of naval air,' and they'd just try to be a little discreet about it. Of course, I overdo in everything: how I mow the lawn, how I paint the house. I got carried away. You can't tell someone who's in the prime of life that their sex drive isn't the be-all and end-all, that in twenty years their relationship will be more important. I had captains tell me, 'You're out of your mind.' And I've got copilots today who tell me they want to leave their wife and their six-year-old kid, and I say, 'Listen. You are out of your mind. Trust me on this.'

"Your mother was blameless. Obviously. She did what she could. She used to call my girlfriends. Actually *call* them. Or their mothers. 'This is Susan Giles.' The whole bit. That was something she got from my mother. She'd go to my mother. She'd say, 'Louise, your son's cheating on me. What should I do?' Of course, my mother would say, 'Kill the son of a bitch.' And your mother would say, 'No, really.' And my mother would think about it, and then she'd say, 'Kill the son of a bitch.' Eventually, they hit upon this phone call thing. In retrospect, it wasn't a bad idea. 'You're screwing my husband' or 'Your *daughter's* screwing my husband.' Excuse my language. Your mother started doing this all the time. A couple of times she called people I wasn't actually screwing, which was awkward, but what the hell. She was fighting.

"And then she *stopped* fighting. She said, 'To hell with him,' which, to be honest, is something she probably should have said a good deal earlier. She divorced me. You may have some recollection of all this, although you were still quite small. What's strange — and this will give you an idea of how skewed my thinking was at the time — what's strange is that I didn't take the divorce seriously. Even when she started seeing other men, I didn't take it seriously. I assumed she was trying to bait me. Follow? Despite all the trouble I'd given your mother, I really did believe in marriage. In the sanctity of marriage. Your mother and I both had the same rose-covered-cottage syndrome. We both — despite all the evidence to the contrary — we both wanted that. The picket fence. The whole bit. So, as I say, I didn't take the divorce seriously. I didn't even see it as a setback.

"The moment your mother began dating Roger Marsh, though, I knew there was going to be trouble. The other men she had dated had been very high tempo. They'd been type-A personalities, which, I'm sure I don't need to tell you, is what your mother and I are. And your sister, needless to say. We're violent type As. But here was Roger Marsh. Roger was a heavy B, as you know. Roger had a completely different point of view. He was a classy guy. He was a 'Courtship of Eddie's Father' guy. Liked the theater and dinner and things of that nature whereas, at that time, I had a gruff way of doing things. I was a drinker, and so forth.

"The real killer, to be honest with you, was that you idolized Roger. I knew I had your sister wrapped around my finger. But you just *idolized* him. Which was perfectly understandable. You were a type B from the day you were hatched. I don't mean that as a put-down — I love Bs. Joy's a B. I *married* a B. Another thing: you were big on baseball at the time and Roger was heavy into sports. I put an airplane in your hands when you were a month old and you threw it out of the crib.

"So you worshiped the ground this guy walked on, and that was the ripper. I could see that if Roger stuck around you'd be gone, and I wasn't going to have that. No goddamn guy was stealing my son. I was constantly at your mother to get rid of Roger. But she wouldn't. Why should she? For once, she had found a guy who wasn't a complete ass, a guy who was genuinely there for her. And she loved it. Your mother and Roger eventually developed some personal problems — she can tell you about that, if she cares to — but for a while, she loved it.

"I used to keep tabs on them. Whenever I was in town, I used to drive over to 10 Gilbert Road. I used to sneak around to the back of the house — I wasn't allowed on the property, see — and I'd just watch them. It'd be dark. The house would be lit up. I'd see Roger and your mother walking around inside. You and your sister. It sounds more sort of Peeping Tom-ish than it was. I just wanted to know what I was up against. I just wanted to know how your mother and Roger's relationship was progressing. And it clearly *was* progressing. I'd see Roger with an apron on. I'd see Roger proposing a toast. Whatever. And

I would basically just sit there in the grass fuming. I'd be livid, but I never left until Roger left.

"One time I got back from the airport very late, and I thought I'd swing by 10 Gilbert Road just for kicks. It must have been 0200. Well, while I was sitting there, your mother came out onto the back porch. I don't know why. To shake out a tablecloth. Something. Well, this was asinine, but I actually whispered something to her. I don't remember what I said. 'Susan.' Whatever. Needless to say — it's two in the morning, she's got her nightgown on — your mother was scared shitless. She bolted inside. A couple of minutes later, Roger came out on the porch. Said, 'Hello? Hello?' That kind of thing. At this point — finding Roger in the house in the middle of the night — I was beside myself. I was ready to jump up and throttle the guy. As if a burglar or a maniac is going to be scared off by a man in jockey shorts. I'm sorry. Roger was a classy guy, but at times he behaved like a moron.

"Well, eventually, they both went back to bed. And I went home. What was I going to do? Hurtle through the French doors? I wasn't quite to that point. So I go home. Fifteen minutes later, two cops knock on my door. They say, 'Are you Glen Giles? Were you at 10 Gilbert Road tonight?' 'I am Glen Giles. I was *not* at 10 Gilbert Road tonight. Are my wife and kids okay?' I thought I'd throw that in. Anyway, one of the cops walks over to the Cougar — remember the red Cougar? 'This your car?' 'That's affirmative, officer.' What was I going to say? Cop puts his hand on the hood. Of course, the hood is still hot. 'You'd better come with us.' 'Do I have to?' 'We'd advise you to.' Well, I wasn't going to argue with a couple of cops. I had a trip the next morning. I had an 0600 get-up, and I flat didn't want to go to jail. So they hauled me down to the justice of the peace. Moore was his name. Good man. I paid a twenty-five-dollar fine, which was better than a sharp stick in the eye, and he let me go. No big deal.

"Once this had happened, though, I more or less stayed away. Jail was not my bag. I did call Roger one time. This was a month or so before they got married — you were an altar boy at their wedding, remember that? That really ticked me off. Anyway, I was on a trip, sitting in a hotel room. I just got on the phone and said, 'Roger, I want you out of there.' I laid down the law. Of course, he told me to fuck off — even 'a B knows when to say 'Fuck off.' It was a ridiculous thing for me to do. I'd gotten the idea from your mother, I suppose. But I figured it was worth a shot. I had tried several different things and that was just one of them. Of course, it didn't fly. Roger — give him some credit — Roger had the wherewithal to say, 'You had your chance,' and hang up. And then they got married, and you were their altar boy."

In November of 1989 — a week before my sister married her longtime boyfriend, Michael — my mother's house on Reservoir Road was overrun by ladybugs. Initially, I was not clear on what had transpired. My mother was so distraught that when she called she'd say only, "They're in everything, Jeffrey. *Everything.*" She would then drop the phone and I'd hear her thwacking a slipper against the kitchen counter. When she picked up the phone again, she'd say, "Got a couple of them. Saw them crawling up the refrigerator. The things are everywhere, Jeffrey. *Everywhere.*"

In the intervening year or two, I have formed this outline of the ladybug episode: My mother wanted to bring a few plants indoors for the winter but was afraid that they might be infested. Her friend Lonnie told her that for a nominal fee the government would send her a box of dormant ladybugs. The ladybugs would kill off her plants' pests and, having completed their mission, expire shortly thereafter. My mother wrote away for the bugs. For a week, they lay dormant in a brown, pastry-style parcel in the refrigerator. A few days later, my mother was carrying the ladybugs out to the garden when the phone rang. She put the box down on a couch and went to answer it.

It was my sister calling. My mother and my sister launched into some last-minute wedding negotiations: Where was Joy going to sit? Who was going to sit with my mother? Etc. This was one in a series of conversations during which my sister would end up shouting, "You're such a wicked bitch" and slam down the phone. Susan would then mix herself a Kahlua and cream and call my mother back. Their next conversation would be appreciably calmer, but my mother would inevitably shout, "Do it your way, Susan. You know so much. Do it your way," and slam down the phone. My mother would make herself a mimosa and call Susan back. And so on. An hour later, they'd be drunk and crying to each other over the phone.

After the last round in this particular conversation, my mother went upstairs, where she watched five minutes of a "Gilligan's Island" rerun before falling asleep for several hours. She woke up at nine in the evening, heated some leftover Chinese food, which she ate from the skillet, spent a few hours billing clients, then went back to bed. Two days later, the ladybugs had taken over the house.

Whenever my mother called to give me an update, she'd insist that I not mention the ladybugs to my father.

"I just don't need it from him right now," she told me on one occasion. "We're still fighting over who sits where and the band and this, that, and the other thing. Joy wants to be in the receiving line. I *will not* stand next to that woman. I'd rather sit in the car."

"What does Susan want?" I asked.

"Susan?" my mother said. "Susan wants *everybody* in the receiving line. She's into this one-big-happy-family horse-shit. I keep telling her, 'Susan, where have you *been?*'"

"Let her do what she wants," I said. "If she wants to ice skate down the aisle let her do it. You're crazy to get yourself worked up."

"I know, I know," my mother said. "You can't win an argument with your sister anyway. Meanwhile, I've got these ladybugs. The exterminator told me they only lived a couple of days, right? He said they'd die and I could just sweep them up. Bullshit. That was two, three days ago. These friggin' things are gonna outlive *me*. I'm supposed to have people over on the morning of the wedding. You know how I do: prosciutto and melon, stuffed mush-rooms. And I've been redecorating like a crazy lady so I don't have to take any condescending b.s. from your father — after all these years that bastard *still* knows how to get to me."

"Don't let him," I said. "He lives for that."

"Believe me, I know," she said. "But how am I gonna entertain here, Jeffrey? Honestly. We're all gonna be sit-ting in St. Anthony's picking ladybugs out of our hair. And I can just imagine what your father and Joy are gonna say about *that*. So I'm in the middle of all this. Plus I've got your sister calling me every five minutes and crying because the band doesn't know 'Stand By Me.' She and Michael have been taking rumba lessons and they want to rumba to 'Stand By Me.' "

"Is 'Stand By Me' a rumba?" I asked.

"Who fucking knows," my mother said. "I told Susan, 'If you want the band to play it they will play it. Or they'll have *me* to answer to.' Listen, Jeffrey, when are you coming up? You coming up on Thursday?"

"Yeah," I said. "By train."

"Jennifer coming?"

"Of course."

"Good, good. Listen, can I ask you a favor? Will you guys sit with me at the reception, honey? I don't have a date 'cause I'm such a fat pig."

I realize that I've said nothing in these pages about my love life. Let us pretend then that Jennifer Bevill, the woman with whom I was to take the Amtrak up to Boston, was the first woman I ever loved. Why not? There are those who will thank me if we do. Let us forget high school, and with it Vickie. Vickie was a flutist. After band practice, when playing the French horn had left my lips purplish and numb and branded them with the faint circumference of a mouthpiece, Vickie and I used to drive to my house, blockade my bedroom door with my bunk bed, and kiss until my mother got home. It was a sweet courtship, although Joe and Alan would occasionally chase us around town in the Bug, sticking their heads out their windows and screaming profanities.

Let us forget college. Let us forget, for instance, Lisa. This will not be easy. Lisa was kind and quiet, and had wide, dark eyes. I loved her because she took it in stride when, during an Easter dinner, my mother went on a crying jag and said, "Excuse me, Lisa, but my children are selfish, ungrateful fucking pigs" and locked herself in her bedroom.

Let us forget Julia. One night, Julia sat in my Brown dorm room and put up with an hour's worth of nervous blather on the subject of R.E.M. (I was trying to romance her and I actually believed that this was the height of seductive patter.) When at last I ran out of breath, Julia put her hands on my hips and said, "Are we gonna have a relationship, or what?"

Finally, let us forget Debra. Debra was spiky and con-frontational, something of a Betty Blue. She spent a lot of time pointing at people and shouting. I admired her for this — I even admired her shabby thrift-store dresses and the way she dirtied the corners of her mouth when she ate — but our relationship was purely damage control from the get-go. One minute Debra would be writing me goofy, childlike love poems and the next she'd be telling me to take my Calvino novels and my acoustic guitar and go fuck myself. Eventually, I did.

I met Jennifer during the waning days of my residence at the Tackiest Apartment on Earth. She was an illustra-tor. Every so often, while I was drowsing behind the recep-tion desk at the high-minded magazine that employed me — a tedious job which, in an effort to keep the pub-lication's startlingly obsessive readership at bay, consisted mainly of denying any knowledge of who worked at the magazine or what they did — Jennifer would materialize on the other side of the Plexiglas partition. Her wire-rim glasses would be pushed high up on her nose, her dyed-black Louise Brooks hair would be swinging, her cheeks would be brushed red with the cold. She would

hand me a pink envelope filled with pen-and-ink draw-
ings of figure skaters, barometers, and Victorian chairs,
and then disappear into an elevator.

When we first started dating, Jennifer was still involved
with someone she had grown up with in Alabama. He was
a waiter — not unhandsome, but bony and thin, with hair
sculpted rather too preciously with styling gel — and he
had followed Jennifer to New York when she set off for art
school. They had been dating on and off for eight years.
Even after Jennifer broke it off with the Waiter, I was
plagued by the fear that she'd return to him. I stayed at
Jennifer's apartment regularly and departing in the
morning I'd leave a conspicuous wake of personal posses-
sions — books, deodorant, shoes, tapes — in an effort to
make my presence in her life seem vast and intractable. I
knew that the Waiter lived nearby, and I thrilled each time
Jennifer hung our laundry — *our* laundry! — out on the
sloping clothesline that stretched over the low, neighboring roofs. I used to imagine that the Waiter would walk by
and, looking up, see my bright blue shirts and floral box-
ers hanging like a row of flags outside Jennifer's kitchen
window. I imagined that when he saw these signs he would
shudder, knowing that he had been unseated and forgotten in this railroad-style, fourth-floor walk-up on Park
and Eighth in Hoboken.

As it happened, the slick-haired Waiter made himself
scarce for a few months and, by the time he finally came
knocking, Jennifer sent him packing. Suddenly, she and I
were in love. I loved strange and disparate things about
Jennifer. I loved the fact that she was from Alabama. I
loved the fact that, while I had been lurching around in
my scratchy marching band uniform, Jennifer had been a

cheerleader. She was mortified about it, but on the not infrequent occasions when I went on a self-congratulatory tear about some freelance article I'd written, she was not above flapping her arms and chanting sarcastically, "Go Jeff! *Push* 'em back. *Push* 'em back. Go Jeff!"

I loved the fact that Jennifer was teaching herself how to swim and owned a pink, Styrofoam, Ten Commandments–shaped flutter board. I loved the Southern tinge to her voice when, after a single beer, she would insist rather hotly that she had Cherokee blood and was distantly related to Wayne Newton. I loved the fact that she had a cat named Earl; that she had a high, escaping laugh; that she collected things made out of tin and blue glass; that she was a terrible but unapologetic cook; that she cut her own bangs to a blunt horizontal even though my sister told her she looked "like a retard"; that every morning she doused herself in baby powder and could always be found at the end of a trail of perfect white footprints.

Even after we had been together for some time, I had moments of insecurity where Jennifer's love was concerned. In desperation, I devised this test: I would wake her in the middle of the night and ask her my name. I was certain that, when her guard was down and she was unhinged by sleep, Jennifer would speak the name of the person she truly, instinctively loved. It was me or the Waiter — there were no two ways about it. So on nights when I couldn't sleep I'd wake Jennifer up and say, "What's my name?" The first few times I tried this her answer was, disappointingly, "Wayne Newton." I would shake her shoulders slightly and she would laugh. I would repeat my question and now, her eyes still pressed together, she would turn toward me, a heavy, sighing weight on my chest, and whisper, almost inaudibly, my name.

The night before Jennifer and I took the train up to Boston, I woke only once and found, by some peculiar and momentary arrangement of clouds, that the room was bathed in a rose-colored light. I fell back asleep. At nine, I awoke in a charitable, John Cheeverish mood feeling that people were basically good and that we learn from everything that happens to us. Jennifer and I made grilled cheeses for breakfast and thought them excellent. We went to the laundry where "You Don't Send Me Flowers" was playing on a dented AM radio and the owner — chubby and stubbled and perched up on a shaking, triple-load washer — was singing the Neil Diamond verses tenderly and in surprisingly fine voice. At one o'clock, we boarded our train and quickly found seats in a quiet, childless, nonsmoking car. Heaven!

I was always in good spirits when Jennifer joined me on my treks home. Her very presence — the presence of someone whom my family hardly knew — urged everyone toward civility, toward normality and decorum. What's more, Jennifer was talkative and inquisitive. When I couldn't stand another moment among my family and went off to lie down in an empty room, Jennifer would pick up the slack and forge ahead in my stead. I felt that I suddenly had a partner in all this.

Upon arriving in Boston, Jennifer and I took the Red Line to Quincy and walked the block or so to my sister's salon. Everyone but Susan had left for the day, and she was in a far corner cutting Joy's hair. My father, wearing his airline uniform and looking older, thinner, and harder in the face than I remembered him, was sweeping up his wife's hair as it fell to the checkerboard floor.

"Just leave it," my sister was telling him as Jennifer and I walked in. "We pay someone to do that."

"You watch what you're doing and never mind about me," my father told her, still sweeping.

"*Leave it*, Dad," Susan said, exasperated. "You're like a little kid. You can't sit still."

"Just watch what you're doing."

"I don't know how you put up with him, Joy," Susan said, groaning and turning back to her work. "He's so aggravating."

"He isn't always like this," Joy said, laughing her British trill of a laugh. "He's just got a lot of energy. He's nervous about the wedding."

"That's right, I'm nervous about how much it's *costing* me," my father said. "I'm never going to retire at this rate. They're going to have to push me to the cockpit in a wheelchair."

"Yeah, right, Mr. Money Bags," my sister said, then turned and saw us. "Jennifer, your *bangs!*"

"Sorry, Susan," Jennifer said, as we all traded handshakes and hugs. "They were getting in my eyes."

"Well, you're not going to my wedding looking like a five-year-old," Susan said. "Sit down. You're next."

"What about me?" I said. "I need a trim."

"Forget it, Willy Wonka," Susan said.

"*I'll* cut your hair, Jeff," Jennifer said, brightening.

"No friggin' way," Susan said, jokingly stabbing the scissors at her. "You touch my brother's hair and *neither* of you are coming to my wedding. Sit down, Jeff. I'll do it. I was only shittin' ya."

"Language, Susan," my father said. He hitched up his creased, regulation gray slacks — revealing smooth and pale bands of calf above his socks — and knelt to retrieve a C-shaped ring of hair that had fluttered beneath the chair. "Are you going to kiss your husband with that mouth?"

"Shit, shit, shit," Susan said. "Now *leave* it, or I'm not cutting *anybody's* hair."

The next morning, after a few hectic but undisastrous hours at my mother's house on Reservoir Road, the wedding party convened at St. Anthony's. At eleven o'clock, my twenty-six-year-old sister, tears coursing freely down her face, negotiated the aisle on my father's arm. Awaiting them at the altar were Michael — shortish and broad, the dome of his scalp beginning to surface through his thinning hair — the priest, and the video cameraman. This last member of the party, who wore a thin, red leather tie and crouched behind a tripod, was as discreet as possible, confining his work to tracking shots of my sister and father and slow, steady pans of the congregation.

Sitting in my tux in the front row, I looked around at the plain, airy church. I had been an altar boy here years before. I remembered arriving early before mass and knocking about in the back rooms. I would spend twenty minutes finding a proper cassock — long cassocks caused me to trip and short ones left my denimed shins awkwardly exposed. I would then start lobbying Father Keohane for permission to work the left side of the altar. The altar boy who worked the left side was a real participant in the Mass. He ferried the bread and wine back and forth between the altar and the sacristy and, at those crucial moments in the Eucharist when the priest raised each in turn toward the heavens, he got to shake the startlingly loud golden bells. The altar boy who worked on the right side merely knelt. He surveyed the crowd for his friends' faces. He tried not to laugh.

Later, during my teens, I went to church only when my mother begged me to. More than anything else, our trips seemed a part of the brave-face strategy with which she approached her separation from my father. My mother would take my arm as we entered St. Anthony's. When she stopped to chat with friends, I would wriggle toward freedom but she would grip my arm with her fingernails, locking me in place. Her face — smiling and nodding in idle suburban banter — never betrayed a sign of the struggle. At last, she'd say her goodbyes and steer me away saying, "Be goddamn nice for once." We'd then slide into one of the cool wooden pews for mass. My mother would clutch her hymnal and sing with her chin up. Bored, I would indulge in adolescent games, such as mentally exchanging the name Jesus for the name Fred. ("And at His right hand sits His only son, Fred," etc.) Once my father and Joy had been sighted at St. Anthony's, of course, my mother stopped going and I was quit of this glorified babysitting. Thus, my religious life skidded to an inauspicious halt.

Now, my sister and my father reached the altar. My father swiveled smartly, militarily, in his tux and turned back toward his pew, the lens of the videocamera in pursuit. Initially, I had been surprised that Susan had not asked both of our parents to give her away. Watching the reluctance with which she released my father's arm, though, I couldn't help but think, These two have been in it together from the start.

I didn't resent this. It struck me that Susan was smarter to have gone through those years aligned with someone rather than no one. If anything, I felt that, by not clinging fast to my mother, I had broken some unspoken agreement. The family had been meant to split into two opposing factions — my father and my sister, my mother and myself — but I had foiled that symmetry. I had stupidly left my mother and me to wander loose in the world. Now, I regretted it, felt a sadness tightening my eyes. On these occasions when I felt a flush of familial love and collusion — Almerinda's funeral, Susan's wedding — the feelings seemed preposterously late. The family had already splintered; we had all sped off in different directions. These feelings, then, came like light from a star — no less bright for the fact that the star had long since gone out.

I looked over at my mother and Jennifer. They had their arms around each other and were crying. Jennifer, her bangs spiky and heavily moussed, was wearing a blue velvet dress and pearls. She was seated beneath a carved wood station of the cross — Christ Falls for the Second Time — and light from the church's great paned windows fell around her. Our eyes met and I gave Jennifer a swooning look meant to indicate how lovely she was. She could not read my expression. She caved her eyebrows in, questioning. My mother, noticing that we were staring at each other, bugged her eyes out cartoonishly and gestured toward the altar. We all smiled.

By now, Susan had stopped crying and her arm was looped through Michael's. Her face, striped here and there with mascara, had an innocent, restful look. It reminded me, suddenly, of the old photograph in which she leans thoughtfully on a fake fence post. From this point in time, that image seemed more reasonable. The world, finally, was slowing down for my sister.

At the reception, there was only one worrisome incident. Susan's friend Karin picked something from the folds of her burgundy bridesmaid dress and said, "Oh, how cute, a ladybug," and my mother replied, too stridently, "Kill it. *Crush* it."

Later, Susan and Michael did a graceful rumba to "Stand By Me." Susan and my father slow-danced, somewhat stiffly, to "Daddy's Little Girl." The rest of the guests poured in around them and the band played "Good Thing," by Fine Young Cannibals, and "I Will Survive," by Gloria Gaynor. The video man weaved from table to table with a microphone, asking guests to say a few words to Susan and Mike. Obliging, the guests, blurry-eyed from beer, squeezed into the frame and said, "Mike, Sue — you guys are awesome" and "Sue, you gotta cut my hair, I'm a freak show."

My mother and father didn't speak to each other. They held forth with their friends in opposite corners of the room, my father in his tux and red bow tie, my mother in her sparkling, flapper-style gown. Watching them, I was struck by how harmless they had become. There had been a time when they could not be in a room together without the air being charged with hostility and expectation. I remembered a morning when my mother, my father, and I were in the kitchen at my mother's house, in Cohasset. I was twelve. I had a fever and I was sitting on the counter in my pajamas while my mother ground down aspirin with the back of a spoon. As a child, I had been terrified of taking pills. Even at an age when I should have been able to swallow them without fanfare, I'd feel my throat contract involuntarily the instant I put one in my mouth. I'd try to wash the aspirin down with water but it would simply teeter at the back of my throat — blocking my windpipe and dissolving into a bitter chalk that made me gag — until I coughed it up again. Now, I remembered my mother crushing a pill, sweeping the powder into orange juice, and watching the white flakes drift like sediment down to the bottom of the glass. She started on a second aspirin but this time the spoon slipped and the pill shot across the room.

My father looked up from his airline schedules and shook his head, disgusted. "He's old enough to swallow the things like everybody else does," he said.

"Don't listen to him," my mother told me, tapping another aspirin out onto her palm.

Soon, this pill too skittered onto the floor. My mother let out a long breath. Before she could draw another aspirin from the bottle, my father stood up in a fierce blur of movement that caused the table to jump. He grabbed the aspirin bottle out of my mother's hand.

"Come here," he told me.

I backed away.

"Come here," he said again. "*Now.*"

I wouldn't move so my father came and pulled me down off the counter. He took my feverish face in the V of his hand and said, "Open."

"But — "

"No discussion. Open."

I looked at my mother.

"Glen — "

"*Open*, goddammit," my father said.

I opened. My father put an aspirin in my mouth. My throat constricted and I could taste the dissolving pill on my tongue. My father released his grip on me and handed me a glass of water.

"Glen, you're a real bastard," my mother said. "Jeffrey, you can spit it out."

"You spit it out and you'll eat it off the floor," my father said.

I took a drink of water and felt the pill bang around at the back of my throat. I began to cry, then choke.

"Swallow it," my father said.

"Spit it out, baby."

"*Swallow* it."

At last, the pill went down. My mother, crying now, smoothed my hair. "You did it, kid," she said.

My father held up a second aspirin. "He's not through *yet*," he said.

Now, at my sister's reception, my father seemed a man incapable of threat or harm. He appeared shy, bright-eyed, slightly rumpled, surprisingly small. His good looks had been dulled, and his yellow-white hair had the thin, swept look of grass which, having grown too tall, bends under its own weight. I saw in him a man who called elderly waitresses "young lady"; who drank chocolate milk; who had begun to call me regularly and always began conversations with "Remember your father?" It was hard — infuriatingly hard — to hold a fifteen-year-old complaint against such a man. Even where his treatment of my mother was concerned, I found it hard to summon up much anger. I had long wanted to believe that some things were unforgivable, that there was right and wrong, that everyone must be held accountable, and so on. Still, looking at my thin, bending, fiftyish father — his head nodding sympathetically, his arm around Joy's waist — who was there to be mad at? And looking at my beaming, gesturing mother — lonely perhaps, but hardly Eleanor Rigby — who was there to be mad *for*?

I sat with Jennifer and watched my parents above the bobbing mob of dancers. Despite the fact that they didn't seem remotely aware of each other, I couldn't help but wait for trouble. At one point, my father headed toward my mother, and I got up and bolted across the room to intervene. As I reached my father, though, I saw he was holding a shiny plate and was actually headed for the banquet tables.

"Hey, son," he said. "Having fun?"

"Sure, Dad," I said.

"Good," he said. "Because this is costing me an arm and a leg."

"You'll live, Mr. Money Bags," I said.

I pivoted and returned to my table, embarrassed that I had scented trouble. Jennifer set her drink down and flapped her arms. "Go *Jeff*," she said. "Hold that line. Hold that line. Go *Jeff!*"

"Michael will never cheat on your sister. If he did, it would crush her. And, of course, she'd have his head for it. She's already warned him. She said, 'If I can't kill you, my father will. And if my father can't kill you, you're going to have to answer to my *mother*.' Your mother certainly tried to stop *me* every way she could. But even after she had divorced Roger and come to Cohasset — that took some doing on my part, as you probably know — I started in with the stewardesses more or less immediately. That's just where I was at. I remember standing you up for dinner once, Jeff. You've probably forgotten. What it came down to, as terrible as it sounds, was that I had a better offer. Pure and simple. I called you and said I couldn't make it. Of course, you said, 'How come?' You said, 'I'm hungry. What do you mean you can't make it?' I felt awful, mainly because I didn't know what to say. I had become so flip about the whole thing — the stewardesses, the screwing around — that I didn't bother to think up excuses.

"After we'd been in Cohasset a couple of years, your mother started seeing Joan Zahn. Do you remember Joan? She was a nasty, nasty woman. Hated my guts, of course. Well, pretty soon your mother got it into her head that therapy could save our relationship. She even dragged me to a couple of shrinks. I went because the relationship *was* important to me. Still. Despite all evidence to the contrary. Despite the fact that I had been fucking up — excuse my language — since time immemorial. People rob banks. They weren't raised to rob banks. They don't necessarily think it's *right* to rob banks. Follow?

"In any case, I went to a couple of shrinks. They were far crazier than I was. One guy was pretty good, but he ended up committing suicide. I'm saying this in all seriousness. He killed himself. Another guy I went to was an utter pig. He used to cut his fingernails during the sessions. I went to him for a month and he cut them every single time. I tried changing the session time, the day of the week. I assumed the man didn't cut his nails eight hours a day, five days a week. Well, apparently he did. Enough said. Q.E.D. That was the end of him. I was dropping fifty bucks an hour and he was giving himself a manicure. He was fussing with his cuticles. So I stopped going to shrinks and that's really when your mother and I called it quits. We were both type As — violent type As — and sometimes that just doesn't fly.

"If Michael started screwing around, your sister wouldn't bother with the shrinks. She'd just kill him. Susan has had my temper since the day she was hatched. I still remember the first time she took a swing at your mother. She was *eighteen months* old. We were driving to a restaurant in New Hartford. A Shakey's Pizza, actually. Your sister was standing up in the back seat and taking swipes at your mother. I was astonished. I pulled over. Turned around. Pushed her down in the seat — not hard or anything because she wasn't even two years old — but I made my point. I said, 'Don't you *ever* hit your mother.' And she didn't. For about five minutes.

"Here was a kid who just had too much energy. Here was a kid who would never go to bed. Your mother and I used to tie her leg to the bedpost. Literally. It sounds like brutality, but it wasn't. The kid needed to sleep. We'd tuck her in at 1800 and she'd come waltzing out five minutes later. It was a game to her. We'd tuck her in a second time. She'd wait five minutes and then she'd be out of bed again. We'd hear her up in her room. She'd be running in circles like an Indian. Susan was hyperactive. That's all there is to it. Of course, we didn't know that at the time. I'm not sure that word even existed. Susan probably needed some sort of special diet. Well, your sister and I always ate candy like it was going out of style. Heath Bars, Snickers. Peanut butter straight out of the jar. Your mother would bake a cake and leave it in the refrigerator. The minute she went to bed, Susan and I would be down in the kitchen fighting over the frosting. The next morning the cake would be a mess and nobody wanted to look at the thing, let alone eat it. That used to tick your mother off something fierce. It ticks Joy off too.

"So Susan was always hyperactive, and obviously the fighting didn't help matters. Those last few months we all lived together in Cohasset were just devastating. As I'm sure you remember. I refused to see any more shrinks. Your mother was downing buckets and buckets of pills. We had just run out of answers. And we'd have some real battles. We'd go at it like there was no tomorrow. Shouting, pitching stuff across the room — the whole bit. And your sister was always standing right there in the middle of it. Just like she had when we were in New Hartford. Just like she had when she was ten. Susan flat couldn't stand to see us fight. She'd always be there trying to break it up, which just made it worse, because now there were *three* of us shouting and pitching stuff across the room.

"You, of course, used to hole up in your room. Perfectly understandable. That's exactly what I did when I was fifteen, or whatever. You had a very strong — and I don't mean this as a put-down — you had a strong survival instinct. You didn't want to get dragged into the battles. You didn't want to get your hands dirty. Your relationship with your mother wasn't bad, I don't think. You didn't particularly care for *me*. Again, perfectly understandable. You were angry. You and I would go driving someplace and you'd just stare out the window. You wouldn't even look at me. You'd answer my questions — you'd mumble and so forth — but you flat wouldn't look at me. And you used to flinch all the time. I couldn't understand that because I never laid a hand on you in my life. In anger, I mean. But you didn't want to have anything to do with me. I could apologize until I was blue in the face, and you'd just nod and stare out the window.

"That was your way of surviving. I realize that that's not much of a revelation, but it took me a long time to figure that out. I used to think about it all the time. Because if you've got a son who doesn't want to have anything to do with you — you *think* about it. You can't help but think about it. So that's the conclusion I eventually came to. You tried to survive by keeping everything inside. Tell me if I'm wrong.

"As for your sister, Susan didn't care if she survived or not. All she knew was that she didn't want to see your mother and me fight — she hated the screaming as much as you did, believe it or not — and she'd kill herself to make us stop. Of course, she *couldn't* make us stop. And maybe that *is* what screwed her up for so many years. You, God forbid, may pay for all this with an ulcer some day. But Susan — I think, I *hope* — has already done her time."

In the summer, Jennifer and I sleep with a fan at the foot of the bed. I'd prefer to run the air conditioner, but Jennifer lives in constant fear of the electric bill. The fan is a tiny concession on my part and I've actually grown fond of the lulling, whooshing sound of the blade. I fall asleep listening to it and, in my dreams, it sometimes appears as a propeller and I imagine that I'm in a plane, rising and sinking through the air.

I rarely have trouble sleeping these days. Sometimes Jennifer does. Sometimes she shakes me awake in the middle of the night. I sit up in bed and our cat, Earl, stands and arches his back. Suddenly, I remember that Jennifer and I have been fighting. Fighting about what? I can't remember exactly. We have been living together for three years and sometimes proximity rubs our nerves raw. I squint at Jennifer. She looks frazzled and sad, illuminated only by what street light finds its way into our room. She has been crying.

"What's the matter?" I say, coming to.

"I can't sleep."

"How come?"

"I don't know. I can't stop thinking."

"About what?"

"You and me. Do you think we're okay?"

"What do you mean?"

"I mean, do you think we're okay? Do you love me?"

"Yes, sweetie. You know I do."

"I've been watching you sleep. You were sleeping so soundly it made me mad. I had to wake you up. Do you hate me?"

"No, no. I'll stay up with you."

"Really?"

"Yes. Of course I will."

"No, you won't. You'll fall asleep. You always do."

"Me? Never. You must be thinking of someone else."

Later — how much later? — Jennifer shakes me again. "You fell asleep," she says, crying. "I was talking and you fell asleep."

"I'm sorry. I just — "

"I don't think it's fair that you should sleep if I can't. I mean, I didn't start this fight."

"Jenny, I can't even remember what we're fighting about."

"Oh, so it's my fault."

"God no. But can't we — can't we talk about it in the morning?"

"I can't *sleep!*"

Jennifer begins crying full force now, her heaving shoulders curved inward. "I'm going to sleep in the living room," she says. She pulls at the top sheet.

"Please don't," I say. "I'll stay up with you. I promise."

"No, I'm going. I don't want to be in the same bed with you."

Jennifer stumbles into the living room. Shortly, she returns and I think she wants to make up, but, in fact, she has only come for the cat. She picks him up. "Come on, Earl," she says and the cat looks at me over Jennifer's shoulder as she whisks him from the room.

I fall back in bed, exasperated, and listen to the metallic creaking of the pull-out bed as she yanks it open. I think about how quickly time lurches forward, how we suddenly find ourselves twenty-five, living with someone, and having vague, circuitous arguments. Life, I think, is like an international flight, during which the hours are compressed to accommodate a time change. They serve you dinner, they let you sleep for two hours, and then they whisk the blinds up for breakfast. One's first reaction is to say, But I've only been asleep for two hours! I just ate dinner! But objections are useless. Morning light is inexplicably pouring in through the jet's round, droopy-lidded windows, and on one's tray table there is the irrefutable fact of a sausage patty and scrambled eggs.

Indignant now, I get up and turn the air conditioner on just to piss Jennifer off. It's a stupid thing to do and I regret it immediately, but not wanting the statement to be wasted, I let it run. In the next room, I can hear Jennifer thrashing in her bed. The pull-out sofa has a horizontal bar that digs into one's back no matter how one arranges one's limbs. Jennifer, I know, can sleep in only one of two positions: splayed out on her stomach with her fists tucked up under her chin, or, if she is having her period and her breasts are swollen and sore, on her side in a tight fetal clench, like a diver doing a cannonball.

Lying in bed, I think, What strange things you learn about a person. What strange things they learn about you. Against your will, you leak out information — stupid, intimate data about your superstitions, your vanities, your insecurities, your hygiene. Your lover knows that from your childhood you retain an admittedly unfortunate habit of sniffing your food; she laughs at a T-shirt you've worn to bed five nights running; she notes the color of your urine and says, "You didn't take your vitamins today." How can you ever leave a person who knows you like this? How can you live with someone for years — bleeding out the petty minutiae of your emotional and biological life — only to walk out one day and start the same slow show-and-tell with someone else? Perhaps when all of your secrets are gone, you feel empty, exposed. You set out to find someone new, but you resolve to be more cautious this time around. You resolve to keep a few thoughts to yourself, to undress in the dark, to close the bathroom door behind you.

Jennifer turns noisily in her bed. I imagine that she has tucked into her cannonball and, picturing her in this attitude, I feel a pang of tenderness. I get up and walk into the living room. It is stiflingly hot and Jennifer's thrashing has left the sheets in a thick, twisted umbilical cord at the foot of the bed. Earl is curled in a crescent against her stomach.

I sit down and brush Jennifer's forehead with the back of my hand.

"Don't touch me," she says.

"Please come back to bed, Jenny. I can't sleep without you."

"Good. Don't *touch* me."

The conversation continues in this vein until, realizing that I am only making matters worse, I go back to bed and stare up at the high, carved ceiling. After a while, Jennifer returns, cradling Earl. She pauses, barely visible, at the edge of the bed.

"We're back," she says, sheepishly trying to make peace. "Earl and I don't like that bed."

"I know," I say. "Come here, sweetie."

"I'm sorry about everything, Jeff. I'm a bitch."

"I'm sorry too. And you're not a bitch. You're a pistol. Please come here."

"You still don't remember what the fight was about, do you?"

"All I remember is that I started it and that it was all my fault."

"That's a good answer. You're learning. He's learning, Earl."

"Thank you. Now, will you *both* come here?"

Soon, Jennifer is asleep, a continent of heat in my arms. A few blocks up there is a Maxwell House factory on the river and a dense, acrid odor settles through the window now. Outside, on the dark street, someone is picking through the trash and a car alarm is sputtering and whining. The noises echo in the canyon of buildings. I cannot sleep. Looking down at Jennifer, her face still bloated from crying, I try to imagine someone else loving her, knowing her as I know her, and I feel another pang of tenderness, this one mingled with possessiveness and jealousy. I will do everything I can to keep her in my life, I tell myself. I will love her purely and without motive. Holding Jennifer now reminds me of the first nights we spent at her apartment, nights when I would lie awake wondering whether she loved me or the Waiter. Outside, a trash can falls over and rolls a distance on the sidewalk. In her sleep, Jennifer's face registers a quick look of alarm. Then, shifting in my arms, her expression relaxes again and, unprompted and with a short, sweet breath, she says my name.

My mother has been dating a Little League umpire named Rob. Her house on Reservoir Road is near the Deer Hill playing field and every so often Rob comes over and raps on the screen door with his face mask. I'm embarrassed to say that I've never been particularly gracious around my mother's suitors. "I'd be having a drink with Gene," my mother will remind me, "and Your Highness would prance in and say, 'Ma, I'm hungry.' Here I am having a drink with a friend, and I gotta put down my glass and say, 'Excuse me, Gene, my sixteen-year-old son needs a grilled cheese.'"

I remember the first time I met Rob. It was not long ago. I took the train to Boston and Joe picked me up at the station. I had come alone — partly because I realized it wasn't fair to ask Jennifer to run emotional interference for me and partly because I wanted to spend all night jamming with Joe. Joe had just graduated from UMass —

it had taken him six years because he kept switching majors — but he was still living at home. He seemed the same as ever except that where he once wore a jean jacket with drumsticks poking out of the front pocket, he now wore clothes he couldn't afford: a white, pressed linen shirt and baggy khaki pants. His hair, once long and stringy, was short, shiny, and layered, and the back of his neck had been stylishly shaved — this my sister's work.

As we drove, I asked Joe how things were and he laughed and said, "Well, Jeff, it's like this — I'm a fucking loser."

"Give me a break," I said.

"No, seriously. I'm a loser. I still live with my parents. I don't have a job. I'd like to get a job in a recording studio or something, but there's no *way* anybody's going to hire me. I had that job at the T-shirt store but I got fired."

"What happened?"

"Long story. I was supposed to do some Spring Break shirts. Rush job. Due the next day. Red ink on white shirts and white ink on red shirts. I don't know what I was thinking about, but I printed a whole bunch with red ink on red shirts. Maybe ten. You couldn't read them. When I realized what I was doing, I was like, 'Oh, fuck. I'm outta here.' I left everything sitting on the counter and I went home and took a nap."

"And your boss got *mad* about that?"

"Yeah, well, he's fussy. Now I'm broke so I can't move out. You know how much money I've got? Seriously. I've got six bucks. Here, look in my wallet."

"How are your parents?"

"They're driving me insane. My mother — she still can't stop picking up the phone. She *lives* to terrorize me. Alan is always calling me from grad school and saying he's giving a poetry reading at a church, or something. And I'm sitting there going, 'Cool. I'd come but I've only got six bucks. I'd come but I'm twenty-six years old and I'm still living with my parents and I'm still a fucking loser.' "

Joe paused and, one hand on the wheel, started carefully rolling up a shirt sleeve.

"You dress well," I said. "I mean, as far as losers go."

"Yeah, I'm still a stud. I'll always have that."

As we entered Cohasset, Joe took the long route to my mother's house, driving along Jerusalem Road, past the statue of the drowned girl, past the sea wall where Camaros crashed, past the cliffs where teenagers jumped into the sea. When we pulled up at my mother's house, Joe left the motor running.

"You don't want to come in?" I said.

"No, thanks. Your mom'll start asking me questions. 'How's your job, Joseph? Where you living?' I don't want to depress everybody."

"OK. We still jamming tonight, Witless?"

"Oh, *dude*. Big time. Hey, do you know that song 'Pearl Necklace'?"

As Joe pulled away, my mother came bustling out onto the porch, the screen door slapping shut behind her. She wore a black silk suit and a thick, braided gold chain. She was barefoot.

"Hi, baby," she said, rushing down onto the grass to hug me. "We were just about to eat."

"Rob's here?" I said. "I'm dying to meet him."

My mother smiled and blushed girlishly. "He's here. You'll be nice, won't you, Jeffrey?"

"Of course, Mom. I just want to check him out. You're awfully young to be dating."

"You'll like him, I think. But just — "

"Just what?"

"Just be a good kid. No baseball jokes, OK?"

"Look at you, you're so nervous."

"I know, I know. It's just— He's the first nice guy I've met in a really long time. The first guy who didn't think I was a crazy lady. So he's a Little League umpire, so what? I don't give a shit *what* he does as long as he's not an asshole."

"Where'd you meet him? Around the batting cage?"

"Don't be a jerk, Jeffrey. No, I— You know, you *meet* people. Your father's not the only one who meets people."

"OK, OK. Let's go inside, Mom."

"I told him all about you."

"Great. Let's go inside."

"You'll be nice?"

"I'll be nice."

"I mean it, Jeffrey. If you love me."

"I love you. Now stand aside."

At last, my mother turned and bounded up the cement steps. Following her, I heard her hum her theme song, that unrecognizable snatch of melody she hums whenever she's nervous. We ducked indoors. The first thing I noticed was that Rob's cleats had left a trail in my mother's Persian rug. We followed the trail into the living room, where Rob was sitting on a couch, absently passing his face mask from hand to hand. My mother introduced us and we shook. Rob didn't seem to know what to say so I said the first thing that came to mind: "Cleats."

A bad opening line. Rob looked down at the tracks in the rug and his face fell.

"Geez," he said. "I'm sorry, Sue."

Rob squatted, and, as if he were dusting home plate, began fluffing up the rug.

My mother, crestfallen, glared at me. "That's all right, Rob, this isn't a museum," she told him with a forced laugh. Then, over his kneeling head, she mouthed, "Be goddamn nice."

My mother sat Rob and me at the dining room table and began carrying plates out from the kitchen.

"You're a writer," Rob said. "You write for magazines."

"Yes," I said, but couldn't think of anything to add. "You're an umpire. You umpire."

"Yes."

My mother set down a tureen of Lobster Newburg and said cheerfully, "Jeffrey used to play Little League. We've got about five thousand copies of *Sports Illustrated* up in the attic."

"I used to worship Graig Nettles," I said, trying to come up with a baseball-related thought.

"Nettles was a good ball player," Rob said.

"Those diving catches," I said.

"*Great* catches," Rob agreed.

"It used to kill me that Brooks Robinson always won the Golden Glove," I said. Where was this coming from?

"Well," Rob said, smiling broadly, "Brooks Robinson was Brooks Robinson."

"You can say that again," I said.

"Brooks Robinson was Brooks Robinson," Rob said, letting out a pair of chuckles not unlike the *glug-glug* that water coolers make.

Rob and I were rolling now. My mother had finished laying the table and was sitting and beaming at us, steam from a basket of bread curling up around her face. Catching my eye, she gave me a bashful, grateful look and I thought for a second that she might cry. Instead, she jumped into our discussion, joking and shaking her hands. A perceptible wave of relief passed over the table, and the three of us started in on a long, easy conversation. The pressure lifted, I sat back in my chair and looked around the house.

Whenever I visit my mother, I wonder at the good work she has done since my father left. From the outside, her house is nothing to look at. It is boxish and covered with bleak, weathered shingles and brown trim — exactly what one expects to find in seaside Massachusetts and points north. Above the front door, one can still discern the outline of a red, white, and blue wooden eagle that had presided there for many years until one day when my mother stood out on the lawn with her hands on her hips and said, "Why have I never noticed that? Susan, Jeff — take the friggin' thing down."

Inside, though, the house is a cool, pale place. It looks, finally, after so many years, like my mother's house. The matching sofas I grew up with — threadbare velvet cushions and carved lion's-paw feet — have long since been replaced. The straw wallpaper — dotted with bald patches where, in boredom, we had routinely picked at it — is gone. My mother's paintings of the barnyard well and the Everglades are gone. The powder-blue rug I used to vacuum is gone too.

My mother's interior design business specializes in Asian antiques and her house is decorated with off-white silk couches, jade-on-blackwood screens, large china Buddhas, and beautiful and fierce figures from the roofs of demolished temples. On the top floor of the house, my mother's most prized possession can be found: an antique Chinese wedding bed. The bed is cherry and ivory, with a canopy perhaps eight feet tall. It is intricately carved and hung with tiny wood-and-rice-paper lanterns. Three years ago, when we visited Hong Kong together, my mother and I sat in a shop for hours, drinking cups of sooty green tea and negotiating with a young Chinese couple for the bed. I had never been so bored in my life, but today it pleases me to think of my mother asleep so high in the house in a bed so elegant and old.

Noticing that my attention was wandering, my mother chimed a fork against her water glass and asked me to say grace. We have been saying the same grace for a dozen years now and, although I don't think I could write it out, I know it phonetically.

"Blesses-o-Lord," I began.

As I said grace, I looked across the table at my mother. Like my father, her looks have faded: she appears as though in soft focus. My mother is tired, but still lovely, with hazel eyes and springy, copper-colored hair.

I looked at Rob the umpire. His forehead was damp and faintly lined with dirt. His face mask had left creases on either side of his face, and pushed his dirty-blond hair up over his forehead in an unnatural wave. Rob's not so bad, I thought. More than anything else, my mother seemed to be looking for someone kind. Someone who'd try to make her happy. Someone who wasn't an asshole.

As I finished grace, I saw that my mother was eyeing me. She likes me to end grace on a personal note — "You know, something *special*" — and she was tilting up her knife and fork, and waiting.

"Mom?" I said.

"Yes?"

"Rob?"

"Yes, Jeff?"

"*Play* ball."

Of all the mislabeled, unwinding film reels that constitute my family's home-movie stockpile, my parents' wedding sequence is one of the few in which my father appears. This does not seem unusual. Home movies have a tendency to be portraits of mothers and children — filmed, as they are, by men. One always sees the same things: Mothers and children by the sides of pools. Mothers and children waking up under quilts at Christmas. Mothers and children on horseback. As a child, a friend of mine, who has since bloomed into a rabid left-winger, was the subject of a hilarious home movie in which she and her mother frolic in identical peach jumpers on what looks to be a red, white, and blue nuclear warhead set in the courtyard of an aeronautical museum.

My father is and has always been an aficionado of gadgetry, infatuated with anything that blinks or beeps or can be made from a kit. It does not surprise me, then, that once he took up the movie camera no one managed to wrest it away from him. He would film a door, then stop the camera, then film Susan or me in front of the door, then stop the camera, and film just the door again. When he viewed the footage, he'd see a figure appear from out of nowhere, then disappear — the kind of no-budget special effect that sends a middle-aged man into paroxysms of laughter and mesmerizes any child who hasn't seen "Bewitched."

Once, when I was thirteen or so, Todd Burke and I were rooting through our cellar when we stumbled upon the black metal box that contains our home movies. Todd and I set up a projector in the living room and viewed them, for the better part of an afternoon, against a white plaster wall. After suffering through one naval training film and a number of black and white "Mighty Mouse" cartoons, we watched perhaps ten birthday parties and half a dozen Christmas mornings. We laughed over the standard items of nostalgia: my tiny plaid sport coats, my sister's constantly flapping mouth, my mother's high and wobbling hair. As time went on, though, we noticed something strange about the films. When my mother was sitting, the camera lingered on her legs; when she was standing, her chest or backside. The same, we noticed to our shared stupefaction, was true of other women who happened to cross my father's line of vision. We were watching a non-stop cabaret of legs and breasts and backsides. Before long, it was impossible to discern what belonged to whom.

"Holy shit," Todd said.

When the camera finally abandoned its prankish swoops and dives, my father's implicit presence was quickly forgotten. We saw only my mother and us children — the various rites of my life whizzing by without any record of my father's participation. My mother seemed to have raised us singlehandedly. She alone seemed to have orchestrated every camping trip, attended every marching band drill, peered with us at every monument between Cape Cod and California. Behind the camera, my father may have been waving and shouting, gesturing us toward the ocean, imploring my mother to hoist us up. None of it appeared on film.

At times, even my memory has holes where my father should be. I know intuitively that he is there somewhere, just as I know he is there when I squint the way he squints and I feel my face become, briefly, his face. Memories of my mother come tumbling out almost against my will: My mother padding out of the house in a pink corduroy robe and helping me start the lawn mower. My mother talking into her tape recorder. My mother eating peppermint patties. The same goes for my sister: My sister fussing over a collage. My sister beating a hammer against my mother's bedroom door. My sister and her husband, Michael, doing a rumba to "Stand By Me."

Where my father is concerned, I often have to reach, to strain, for memories. I suppose this is partly because he just wasn't around a lot of the time. But I suspect it's also because of the fact that — during the years when I felt he should be punished for his absences, for his wanderings, for Joy — I erased him a little bit. Today, typing these words in my bright, wide room, hearing Jennifer shuffling about next door, I reach for a memory, something I would preserve in a home movie if I could.

I find this: I am eight years old and flying in a plane. I have just woken up and the seat next to me is empty. I look around frantically but don't recognize anyone. My stomach tightens in a rush of fear. Suddenly, the intercom above me crackles and a voice comes through the cabin. The voice says, "This is Captain Giles speaking. We're making our descent." Everyone looks up, as if there is something to look at, but there is only the voice. The voice says, "We'll be on the ground in just a couple of minutes."

Everyone listens, but suddenly, magically, the voice is talking only to me and I'm surprised the others can hear it. "We're flying over 10 Gilbert Road, Tiger," the voice says. "If you look out your window, you can see a blue house."

These days, one can have one's home movies transferred onto videotape. One can also have music dubbed onto them — the most common programs offered, I understand, are classical, big-band, and soft-rock hits. Leaving aside the puzzling question of how one chooses the most suitable sound track for one's life, I wonder how music would alter the films. What would it be like to see my mother guide Susan and me down a beach if the image was accompanied by a few minutes of Schubert, or some old Simon and Garfunkel song? Would it be too sad to watch? Would it make me miss my father — or hate him? In the end, I think, the best way to watch the movies is the way Todd Burke and I watched them on the wall that afternoon: sitting in silence with the speckled beam of a Bell and Howell shooting above our heads. One sees images that are already ancient — light sent from a dead star. One hears only the projector, clicking along like a train. And then the last length of film flies out of the machine with a sudden *tap-tap-tap* and once again the wall goes white.